"So what do you suppose is on the menu for dinner?"

Nick murmured the question, his face cradled against Samantha's breast. Her scent was all around him, driving him crazy.

"You," she whispered into his ear.

"Is that all you ever think about?" He tried to sound disapproving, but his voice was warm with pleasure, and his arms held her tight.

"All I ever think about," she agreed, moving invitingly against him. "Well?" she continued, "do I get you?"

Yes, he wanted to say. *Yes, you get me. For always. Forever. Till death do us part.* But the words stuck in his throat.

"Yes, you'll get me, you hussy," he said, releasing her slowly. "But not right now. My aunt is waiting for us to join her for dinner."

Samantha smiled in that irresistible way of hers. Running her hands through his thick hair, she pulled him back to her. "If we hurry, we won't keep her waiting too, too long...."

Candace Schuler, one of Temptation's most popular authors, has done it again with one of her most polished and passionate stories to date. *Sophisticated Lady*'s heroine is a woman of the world, like Candace herself. Here, Candace has made use of her extensive travel experience in the most delightful way. So for those who like glitz and glamor, an exotic and romantic locale . . . as well as a dark, handsome hero, *Sophisticated Lady* has it all.

Books by Candace Schuler

Sophisticated Lady
CANDACE SCHULER

Harlequin Books

TORONTO • NEW YORK • LONDON
AMSTERDAM • PARIS • SYDNEY • HAMBURG
STOCKHOLM • ATHENS • TOKYO • MILAN

To that small but rowdy faction of the RWA
unofficially known as the Bawdy Broads;
this one's for y'all.

For the bitch sessions that last until two a.m.,
for the three-hour lunches at El Chico's,
for the movies and books
I might otherwise have missed,
for the commiseration when I think
I'll never finish another blankety-blank book,
for the sincere words of praise when I do,
but most of all,
for the friendship.

FORTY YEARS OF
Romance

Published August 1989

ISBN 0-373-25361-3

1

THE LITTLE SHIVERS of anticipation dancing its way
down Samantha Spencer's elegant spine was the only
thing that kept the party from being a dead bore. That
and the lavish buffet table. It was decorated in rich emerald green and sparkling silver to match the packaging for Gavino Industries' new line of *Sophisticated
Lady* cosmetics and was loaded down with a tempting
array of mouth-watering pâtés and imported crackers,
a dozen different kinds of canapés and an indecently
large crystal bowl of iced caviar with all the proper ac-
coutrements. Samantha's mouth hadn't stopped salivating since she'd caught sight of it.

She glanced around, wondering if anyone would
notice if she helped herself to another canapé. The other
guests were all standing around, chatting quietly as they
pretended not to watch the closed door at the far end
of the conference room. The scene reminded her of a
gathering of friends and relatives in a church, waiting
for the bride to appear.

But in this case, it wasn't the bride who was late. It
was the groom. Although *groom* wasn't exactly the
right word. Nick Gavino was more like the father of the
bride, she decided, because the new *Sophisticated Lady*
line was definitely his baby. A whimsical little smile
tilted up the corners of her perfectly made-up mouth,

defining the hollows beneath her finely sculpted cheekbones. Did that make *her* his baby, too? she wondered. And, if it did, was that going to be a comfortable thing to be?

She tried to form a mental picture of her new boss and failed. She'd only seen him once, if you discounted the newspaper clippings that her mother had sent her, and the circumstances hadn't been conducive to getting a good long look at the man. There had been lots of bright lights in her eyes, and a great many people milling around, and she'd been very nervous on that most important day in her career. Too nervous to pay much attention to anything but the depressing gorgeousness of her competition.

All that she'd retained of him was an impression of height and darkness, an air of rather formidable power and the unexpected sound of a rich vibrant laugh, which may not have even been his. Probably wasn't his, given the other impressions she'd gotten. The dichotomy had left her with a niggling little desire to see him again, just to find out which of her fleeting impressions had been the real one.

But was he ever going to show up?

Samantha sighed impatiently, absently smoothing her hand over the heavy blond coil twisted into an elegant chignon at the back of her head. Then she leaned forward, reaching around her stepbrother and roommate, Robbie Lowell, toward the temptations of the buffet table.

"Bor-ing," she sing-songed in Robbie's ear as her long fingers deftly snagged a canapé. It was stuffed with some frothy green goo that looked as if it might be avocado and topped with a tiny pink shrimp. "Food's good, though," she added, popping it into her mouth.

"These things are always boring. I think it's a law or something." Robbie slapped at her hand as she reached past him again. "You've had six of those things already," he admonished.

"So?" Samantha scooped up a healthy dollop of caviar with a little crystal spoon and plopped it on a cracker.

"So no one else has had any yet, and you're making a big empty space on the tray. The caterers will have a fit when they see how you've messed up their masterpiece."

"Robbie, this stuff is meant to be eaten, you know. It's not just here to look at. Besides—" she licked a bit of caviar off the tip of one finger "—I'm starving."

"So what else is new?"

Samantha bent her arm at the elbow and discreetly punched him in the ribs. She was surprisingly strong, despite her fragile appearance, and Robbie gave a soft "oomph" as the air rushed out of his lungs. He straightened quickly, reaching out to retaliate with a punch of his own.

"Uh-uh. Not now." Samantha adroitly sidestepped him, motioning toward the door that was opening at the other end of the long conference room. She tugged at the peplum waist of her fitted black suede jacket, straightening it. "I think the festivities are about to begin," she said, the little shivers of anticipation returning full force.

Robbie's head whipped around. "So he's finally decided to make an appearance. It's about time."

"Oh, don't be tacky." Samantha rebuked him mildly, forgetting that she'd been suppressing her own impatience a moment ago. "He probably had some terribly important long-distance call that he couldn't get away from. I'm sure he didn't mean to keep everybody waiting."

She smiled slightly as she spoke, her wide, cool gray eyes drawn to the man who had just come into the room. He stood with his hand on the doorknob, head cocked slightly as he looked back at someone who was in the office he'd just come out of.

Her first impression of height and darkness hadn't been wrong. He stood six foot three, at least, and his skin was a deep golden color that owed nothing to the sun, she decided, and everything to his obviously Latin ancestry. His profile—a strong chiseled nose, angular cheekbones, firm sensuous lips, and an even firmer chin—was classically Italian. It brought to mind the ancient Roman coins she'd seen once at the Metropolitan Museum, the ones stamped with the likeness of some Caesar or other. He held himself like a Caesar, too, and she immediately wondered what he'd look like in a toga.

Judging by the way he looked in a tailored business suit it would probably be a sight to see. She approved of the way the fine charcoal-gray cloth of his suit draped over his tall, powerfully built body. The jacket fell smoothly from the line of his broad shoulders, the pants fit well without being tight, the vest was only just snug enough to hint at the hard torso beneath it. He was obviously not a man who felt the need to advertise. She liked that. She also liked the crisp white shirt that contrasted so nicely with his tawny complexion and the striped silk tie in varying shades of gray and burgundy.

Yes, her first impression had been right, she decided with a small nod of satisfaction; Nick Gavino was an altogether formidable man. Just standing there, he radiated a quiet kind of strength and authority that was all the more powerful for being spoken in whispers. So, could such a formidable man be the same one who had left her with the memory of that rich vibrant laugh? She felt strangely compelled to find out.

"Mr. Gavino is much too suave to keep a roomful of people waiting on purpose," she said to Robbie then, drawing him down the length of the buffet table to the group gathering at the other end. "He's too sophisticated. Too—" one hand fluttered in the air as she searched for just the right word to describe what she meant "—too, oh, courtly. You know? He has a sort of bred-in-the-bone gentility that precludes deliberate rudeness."

"Noblesse oblige," Robbie said.

"Robbie," Samantha began, a touch of exasperation coloring her clear, cultured voice. "I swear, you're beginning to sound like my mother. Mr. Gavino is undoubtedly a very nice—Oh, never mind." She swatted his arm affectionately. "I'm on." A radiant smile turned up her perfect lips at the corners, and she extended a graceful hand toward the tall, dark man who held his hand out to her.

"Miss Spencer." Nick took her offered hand, enclosing it in the hardness and warmth of his. Her fingers were slim and cool, and she was as beautiful as he remembered. No, he corrected himself instantly, she was *more* beautiful than he remembered.

Her skin had a translucent quality, as if light had somehow been trapped beneath its alabaster surface. Her bone structure was heartbreakingly pure; the angled line of her jaw sharp and clean, her nose small and straight, her chin slightly pointed. Her brows arched sharply over wide-spaced gray eyes. Her high cheekbones were just a tad too wide, giving her face that small imperfection necessary for real beauty.

"Welcome to Gavino Industries," he said, smiling down at her. His eyes looked directly into hers as he spoke. They were warm and welcoming and devastatingly sexy.

Much too sexy for someone who looked as formidable and businesslike as he did, Samantha thought. Images of warm starlit nights and rumpled satin sheets were suddenly running riot through her head.

"I'm very pleased to meet you in person at last," Nick said when she remained silent.

Samantha nodded in agreement, a slightly bemused expression on her face as she continued to stare up at him. He would be irresistible when he laughed, she decided. With those hot-coffee eyes of his crinkling up at the corners. And that mouth . . . Oh, he had a beautiful mouth—clean-edged, masculine, inherently sensual. Without effort, she imagined that mouth curving upward in intimate male laughter—imagined those hard masculine lips parting to taste her own.

"Miss Spencer?" he prodded, wondering what was going on behind that remote gray gaze. His Sophisticated Lady wasn't going to turn out to be, well, slow, was she? A lack of brain power would be a crime in such an elegant woman. "Miss Spencer?"

"Hmm?" Samantha refocused her eyes to find her new boss staring down at her with a quizzical expression on his face. She colored slightly, disconcerted at the direction her thoughts had taken. "I, ah . . . Thank you, Mr. Gavino," she managed, silently thanking her mother for all the lessons in proper deportment and ladylike self-control that had been drilled into her. "It's a pleasure to meet you, too." The smile she offered with her words was wide and real, if a bit dazed.

It dazzled him with its brilliance, charmed him with its touch of playfulness, seduced him with its warmth. "Please—" He put his other hand over the top of hers where it lay in his grasp, deciding she wasn't slow at all. Or, if she was, he didn't care. "—Call me Nick."

His voice was deep and melodious, retaining the cadence of his mother tongue without the slightest trace of an accent. It flowed over Samantha's nerve endings like warm honey.

"You're part of our family now—so to speak," he said. "Isn't she, gentlemen?" he asked without even glancing toward the group of businessmen standing to his right. "We don't stand on ceremony here."

Someone snorted in amused disagreement but neither Nick nor Samantha paid any attention. They were too busy staring at each other.

"Nick," Samantha agreed, still smiling up at him. "And you must call me Samantha. Or Sam. Or Sammie." She shrugged, one elegant shoulder moving under the soft suede of her jacket in an unconsciously seductive gesture. "Whichever you prefer."

"Samantha, then." Her name rolled off his tongue as if he were tasting it. "I like that very much. It's unusual but not outrageous. Elegant and sexy. Very ladylike." He squeezed her slender fingers approvingly. "Exactly the image I wanted for my Sophisticated Lady."

"Oh, dear." Samantha's gray eyes flashed with sudden amusement and she tilted her head, looking up at him from under her lashes. "I hope you don't expect me to live up to that."

"Live up to what?"

"The ladylike image." Her expression was both flirtatious and comically distressed. "My mother would say it's impossible."

An eyebrow lifted. "Impossible?" he said, intrigued.

"Oh, definitely. Mother's spent the better part of the past twenty-five years trying to pound some ladylike decorum and refinement into me." She grinned up at him, her sparkling eyes inviting him to share her amusement. "But it didn't work."

The corners of his beautiful mouth quirked upward in answer. "Didn't it?"

Samantha shook her head and leaned forward as if to share a secret.

Nick bent his head, unconsciously pulling her closer by the hand he still held clasped in both of his.

"I'm an unrestrained hooligan," she admitted sotto voce.

Nick laughed. His lips parted slightly, showing a glimpse of white even teeth. His chin lifted a bit, exposing the strong line of his throat. His eyes crinkled up at the corners.

Samantha was delighted. "I *knew* I could make you do that sooner or later," she crowed.

"Make me do what?" he asked, his eyes still smiling at her.

"Laugh. I heard you laugh at the final interviews," she explained. "At least, I thought it was you. But I wasn't sure until now. You have a wonderful laugh." She lifted her free hand as she spoke and touched the corner of his mouth lightly, approvingly.

It was a typical gesture for Samantha—warm, spontaneous and unreservedly friendly. She would have touched another person in exactly the same way had the circumstances been the same, and thought nothing of it. But Nick tensed, the tiny muscles around his mouth going rigid under her fingertips. His pupils darkened. His nostrils flared slightly as he caught the scent of her perfumed wrist.

Samantha's eyes widened, too, and she went as still as he had. And then, seemingly of their own volition, her fingers drifted fractionally, feathering along the edge of his upper lip. "You should laugh more often," she said softly.

Nick stood there for a scant second more, as still as a statue under her touch, and thought of cool satin sheets and shadowed rooms and her slim, elegant hands running over his body. He thought of long, sleepless, sweaty nights and sun-dappled Sunday mornings spent in bed. He thought of the extra-long couch in his office and wondered how she would look stretched out, naked, against the butter-soft burgundy leather.

And then good sense returned, and he gathered himself together, reaching up to grasp the slender hand that was still touching his mouth. Tucking her fingers into the crook of his arm, he turned her to face the room. "Ladies and gentl—" he paused and cleared his throat "—Ladies and gentlemen," he said again, his hand covering hers where it lay on his arm. "I give you Miss Samantha Spencer. Gavino Industries' new Sophisticated Lady."

Samantha smiled and inclined her head, automatically acknowledging the smattering of polite applause, but her mind was numb and her fingertips were tingling from the hard, quick kiss he'd pressed on them just before he'd pulled her hand away from his lips.

"I STILL DON'T LIKE the way he looks at you," Robbie said stubbornly, pushing open the door to their Greenwich Village loft with his elbow, his arms full of grocery sacks.

"Oh, Robbie, really." Samantha spoke over her shoulder as she headed toward the kitchen. "Don't be such a dope." She set her own sacks down on the butcher block counter. "Nick Gavino is our boss now, and for the kind of money he's paying me he can look at me any way he wants to. And besides—" she waved a bunch of carrots at him before she opened the refrigerator door to put it away "—he didn't look at me like *that* anyway."

Robbie shook his head. "He looked at you like you were a piece of prime beef with a For Sale sign around your neck."

"Oh, he did not." Samantha was becoming just a bit exasperated; they'd been arguing about Nick Gavino's intentions toward her all the way home. "He didn't look at me any differently than he did at anybody else." He had, but she wasn't about to go into it with Robbie.

"Well, I still think—"

"Let's just drop it, okay?" She reached out and brushed back the hair from his forehead with a quick, maternal gesture. It did no good. Robbie's light brown hair was wild and wiry by nature, and no amount of brushing, let alone Samantha's slim fingers, had ever tamed it.

It made him look like some fanatical revolutionary type, she thought fondly, the way all those wiry curls framed his thin face and his light hazel eyes. Eyes that were usually lit by something feverish and visionary from within. Now, however, they were filled with a particularly boyish sort of bad temper. It made him seem much younger than the twenty-three he was—and made her feel much older than twenty-five.

"Why don't you open that bottle of champagne we bought and take it into the living room?" She ruffled his hair then withdrew her fingers to finish putting away the groceries. "I'll join you as soon as I finish in here, and we can really start to celebrate, okay?"

"Well—" he drew the word out "—okay." He got two juice glasses from the cupboard, filled one and set it on the kitchen counter for Samantha. "But I still think he looks at you as if you are a piece of meat," he shot back over his shoulder as he went into the living room.

Samantha shook her head, smiling to herself. What Robbie failed to understand was that, in a way, she *was* like a piece of meat to most of the people who hired her. Prime meat, perhaps, but still meat, displaying herself for their approval. It didn't mean anything, and it didn't bother her in the least, because Samantha Spencer was a woman well aware of her own worth.

It wasn't conceit but a healthy self-confidence and respect for herself as a total person that enabled her to feel that way. Without that self-confidence she wouldn't have lasted two minutes in the cut-throat world of modeling. Especially since her "look" wasn't the one that was currently considered hot.

Unlike the wholesome, sexy, all-American golden girl sort of glamour that was typical of a supermodel like Christie Brinkley, Samantha's professional persona was one of cool sophistication. Her ice-blond hair, huge gray eyes and pale, ivory complexion made her perfect for conveying everything from the remoteness of a convent-bred schoolgirl, to a high-society debutante, to the kind of icy sexuality and drop-dead glamour that had surrounded the movie queens of the twenties and thirties. But it didn't make for a modeling superstar.

Until now.

The *Sophisticated Lady* campaign could make her a superstar. Which meant, essentially, that Nick Gavino could make her a superstar.

And Robbie was wrong. Nick hadn't looked at her as if she was meat on the hoof. On the contrary, he'd looked at her as if she were a unique and very desirable woman. The thought gave her goosebumps.

"You'd better get in here before I drink all this stuff by myself," Robbie hollered from the other room.

"Coming," Samantha answered, deliberately putting the thought of her new boss and her reaction to him firmly out of her mind. Picking up her half-empty glass, she hurried into the living room. Nudging a large floor pillow into place with her foot, she sank down onto it on the other side of the coffee table from Robbie and reached for the champagne bottle.

"Well, here we are." She sighed happily and topped off the champagne in her glass. "And here's to us and the new Sophisticated Lady and Gavino Cosmetics and to Mr. Nick Gavino himself," she said expansively, her luminous gray eyes sparkling no less than the liquid in her glass. She tossed back a swallow before she realized that her stepbrother wasn't drinking with her. "Come on, Robbie, drink up. This is a celebration."

"I don't think I want to drink to that Gavino character."

A slight frown wrinkled her forehead. "Are you going to start that again?"

Robbie fixed her with a sulky stare.

Apparently he was. Samantha sighed and lowered her glass. Sometimes, she thought, these creative geniuses were just a bit *too* temperamental. And she didn't exactly feel like soothing the artistic ego today. They were supposed to be celebrating.

But Robbie was one of her best friends, as well as her stepbrother and roommate, and maybe—just maybe— he'd seen something in Nick Gavino's sexy brown eyes that she hadn't. He was always saying that she was too trusting for her own good, wasn't he? On the other hand, she was always telling him that he was too suspicious. It usually evened out in the long run.

"Look," she said placatingly, her smile emphasizing the sculptured cheekbones that were soon going to be the envy of every woman in America. "Just ignore the way you think he looks at me, okay? What does it matter, anyway? It's harmless." She shrugged and took another sip of her champagne. It wasn't nearly as good as the brand that had been served in Nick Gavino's conference room, but what could you expect for six dollars? "Besides, we'll probably hardly ever see him after today." She tried not to let the thought depress her.

"Didn't your agent tell you?"

"Tell me what?"

"Your harmless Mr. Gavino is going to be in Europe while we're shooting!"

Excitement tingled along her nerve endings. "So?" she said, trying to ignore it.

"Is that all you can say? So? Don't you realize what that means, having Gavino coming around on location?"

"No." She opened her eyes wide. "What does it mean?"

"It means that he'll be sticking his nose into everything, that's what it means! He'll want to approve clothes, locations—" He threw up his hands. "Oh, you know what a pain in the ass clients can be. And he'll be worse than most. A chemical engineer." He snorted. "Messing with my shots!"

"Ah-hah!" Samantha crowed triumphantly. "Now we come to the real reason for your hostility for poor Mr. Gavino. You're afraid he'll mess up your precious pictures."

Robbie drew his brows together. "Not funny."

"Mr. Gavino is the client," she reminded him. "He has a terrific amount of money invested in this thing. Millions." She paused for a minute, thinking happily of her own really spectacular contract. She found she couldn't be even the tiniest bit suspicious of the man who had made that possible. "He probably just wants to make sure that everything goes exactly right. I know I would if it were my money."

"It's not his money personally. It's Gavino Industries' money."

"That's splitting hairs, Robbie," she reproached him. "Even though he's the majority stockholder of Gavino Industries, he still has to answer to a board of directors, you know. From what I've heard, he had a really tough fight with them to get the funds for the new cosmetic line in the first place." She leaned across the table. "Word has it that he had to personally guarantee the financing. So, I'd say that makes it his money, wouldn't you?" She eyed him imperiously, suddenly looking every inch the haughty New England lady that her mother had tried so hard to make her. "He's perfectly within his rights to want to oversee things personally."

"Yeah, maybe," Robbie agreed. "But I still think that all he wants to oversee personally is you."

"Oh, Robbie, don't be an idiot."

"And I don't think you'd object much, either."

Samantha laughed. "Maybe not," she agreed. *Definitely not*, she thought, feeling that tiny thrill of anticipation, stronger now, dance up her spine again. "But don't worry," she said then, seeing that he was still frowning. "I can handle Mr. Gavino." *If I get the chance.* She edged his glass across the table and tipped hers toward him, silently coaxing him to drink with her. "Come on, Robbie," she urged sweetly. "Let's drink to us and fame and fortune, and we'll forget all about Nick Gavino." *For now*, she amended silently. "Okay?"

"Okay." Robbie picked up the drink and sipped at the bubbling liquid. Samantha did likewise, smiling approvingly at him over the rim of her glass.

She looked young and giddy, sitting there on the floor, and nothing like the glamorous pictures that Robbie had taken of her to get the *Sophisticated Lady* deal. She had discarded her fitted black suede jacket and matching pumps in the kitchen. The hem of her red silk blouse had been pulled free of her waistband and the legs of her slim black pants were hitched up to facilitate her cross-legged position. Her heavy blond hair had slipped partway out of its pins to hang in wisps around her face and shoulders, framing the grin of pure happiness that lit up the sculptured oval of her beautiful face. A far cry, indeed, from the poised and polished and sophisticated woman who had attended the party in Nick Gavino's penthouse conference room.

"Just think of it, Robbie. London, Paris, Rome. The whole darn world. Can you believe it?" She downed her remaining champagne in one big swallow and fell backward to lie full-length on the bright square of fake oriental carpet with her arms flung out at her sides. "All that just to sell makeup. I love it!" She looked up at him. "Don't you just love it?"

He nodded, smiling at her.

"Good. Give me some more champagne."

She sat up to accept the drink he poured for her. "You know the first thing I'm going to do?" she said, turning the straight-sided juice glass in her hands. "I'm going to buy us some honest-to-goodness real crystal wine-glasses."

"I thought you didn't like things like that. You said your mother's—"

Samantha waved him to silence. "My mother's crystal is that old, heavy, cut-glass kind. I think her great-grandmother brought it over on the Mayflower or something. Mine will be brand-spanking-new crystal. Swedish. Very light and modern." She looked up from under her lashes and grinned impishly. "Mother'll hate it."

She took another sip of her champagne and ran the flat of her hand over the surface of their refurbished coffee table. "The second thing I'm going to buy is a new coffee table. One of those really modern ones made of chrome and glass."

"That kind of thing would look just perfect in here, wouldn't it?" Robbie scoffed.

Samantha looked around the room before answering. It was painted basic white, its walls rising to a maze of blue-painted pipes and air-conditioning ducts in the ceiling fifteen feet above their heads. It was decorated with lots of colorful theater and travel posters. The shining hardwood floor was bare except for the large square of carpet that defined the living area. The tall oblong windows were undraped, but they were filled with a living curtain of blooming, trailing plants that filtered the light and provided privacy. The furniture, a second-hand white wicker sofa with blue and yellow cushions, four canvas-backed director's chairs and stacks of brightly colored floor pillows, wasn't exactly out of *House Beautiful* but it was cheery and comfortable. The coffee table of her dreams would fit in just fine.

She said as much to Robbie.

"Next thing you'll want is to move uptown."

"And live in a cracker box? Don't be ridiculous. I'm going to stay right here in this big lovely loft and redecorate a little. Get a real oriental carpet." She waved her arms expansively. "And some regular chairs—ones with padding and upholstery. Maybe a new stereo set."

"Playing Lady Bountiful, are we?"

"What do you mean by that?"

"You can afford all that," he said in an effort to bring her down to earth. "I can't."

"That doesn't make any difference, Robbie." Her eyes were wide and unconsciously appealing as she stared across the table at him. "You know it doesn't. Share and share alike, remember?"

"Yeah, sure." He downed his remaining champagne. "One for all and all for one."

"Yes, that's right. Besides, you're not exactly poverty stricken these days," she reminded him. "You signed with Gavino Industries, too."

"Yeah, maybe," he agreed, "but taking pictures is a lot less profitable than having your picture taken. And my contract isn't for two years like yours; it's six months with an option if they like my work," he grumbled, reaching for the champagne bottle.

Samantha leaned forward and put her hand on his arm. "You aren't going to spoil this for us, are you?"

Robbie looked at her for a long moment. "No, I'm not going to spoil it," he said with a sigh. "I just wanted to warn you, that's all."

"Consider me warned, then." She patted his arm and sank back on her heels.

"Yeah, well—" He lifted the champagne bottle by the neck. "You want any more of this?"

Samantha shook her head. "Why don't we go out to dinner?" she suggested. "We could go to Angelo's and pig out on his lasagna. Sound good to you?"

Robbie brightened. Angelo's was "their" restaurant. "Sure."

"Okay. I'll go change, then." She pushed away from the coffee table and stood up, already reaching for the buttons on her red silk blouse as she headed toward her room.

Fifteen minutes later she had freshened her makeup and was dressed more comfortably in a pair of soft, clinging black leggings and flat-heeled half boots, topped with an oversized fuchsia and black sweater that hung halfway down her slender thighs. Pulling out hairpins, shaking her head as the weight of her hair was released, she reached for the brush on her dresser. Her hand was stayed by the untidy pile of newspaper clippings scattered over its surface.

Her mother had sent her the clippings shortly after Samantha had announced that she had a good chance of getting the *Sophisticated Lady* contract. The phone call had come first, though, making it clear that while the painfully proper, staunchly WASP Margaret Spencer was obviously pleased that her beautiful daughter was finally achieving success in her chosen career, she was just as obviously distressed at the people Samantha had to come into contact with to achieve that success.

"The family has money, of course, but they're really not our kind," Margaret Spencer had sniffed, implying that the Gavinos were nouveaux riches and, therefore, uncultured and, quite possibly, couldn't be trusted to know which fork to use.

As if, Samantha had thought, the Spencers were any kind of riches at all, despite their pedigreed New England background.

"You must be sure to conduct yourself circumspectly at all times," her mother had continued. "They're Italian, you know, my dear. Not, of course, that I have anything against Italians. They're a very commendable race, for the most part. Michelangelo was Italian. But they are, well, you know, dear, they do have such *extreme* appetites and then—" her voice had dropped to a scandalized whisper, "—there's the Mafia."

It was all that Samantha could do not to laugh out loud but she held her tongue, listening to all her mother's dire warnings with little more than mumbled sounds that could pass for agreement.

The photocopied newspaper and magazine clippings had arrived a few days later. Most of them over fifteen years old, they detailed the goings on of the infamous Gavino family. That had been her mother's exact word—*infamous*. Morbidly fascinated, Samantha picked up a faded clipping and reread it.

Nick Gavino was no more than eighteen in the grainy picture. The line of his beautiful mouth was heartbreakingly young and tender and it was obvious from the way his jaw was set that it took all his willpower to keep his lips from trembling. A woman with her arm in a sling, identified as his mother in the caption, stood at his left side. Her widow's veil was gossamer thin, revealing the perfection of her features and the look of pleading in her dark, eloquent eyes as she gazed up at her tall son. But his head was turned away from her, repudiation in every line as he gave his attention to the little girl clutching his right hand.

She was no older than five or six, with the same soft dark eyes as the woman on Nick's other side, and long dark braids that hung almost to her waist. Her little face was white and pinched and frightened, and she seemed to be hanging on to her brother's hand for dear life. The man they were mourning was their father, shot in the head by his own hand, the news story said, after he had wounded his wife and her lover, Broadway actor Maxwell Peyton.

The next article, dated two months later, announced the marriage of Lucia Gavino, widow of the recently deceased Antonio Gavino, to her lover: "Maxwell Peyton and bride number three, the luscious Lucia Gavino, will be honeymooning in Monte Carlo," Samantha read, "before returning to New York to begin rehearsals for Peyton's new play, *Bank Notes*. Will the third time be the charm, Max?"

Samantha gave an unladylike snort and dropped the article on the dresser, automatically reaching for the next clipping. Dated only eight months after the wedding, it chronicled the messy divorce of the Peytons. There was a picture of the "Luscious Lucia," looking somewhat less than luscious and more than a little furious as she emptied a bottle of wine over the head of her soon-to-be ex-husband and his latest indiscretion.

"Will Lucia Liquidate?" asked the headline in bold, black letters. Further news stories revealed that she would.

What amazed Samantha—other than the fact that anyone other than Lucia's family cared what she'd done—was that *her* mother had actually been able to dig up the old gossip columns. That she would have wanted to didn't surprise her daughter at all. For all her New England propriety Margaret Spencer never forgot a scandal. The juicier, the better. Samantha supposed it made her mother feel morally superior to the people involved in them.

The remaining clippings were more recent and far more mundane. There was a short article about Nick's younger sister—the little girl in the funeral picture— being sent to the family villa in Italy to recover from an unnamed illness. And one showing Nick with a rather elegant blonde on his arm at the opening night of the opera. And another announcing the fact that he had funded some sort of halfway house in the Village. And one that—

"Hey, hurry up in there," Robbie demanded, pounding on the door. His voice was slightly slurred from all the champagne he'd imbibed.

Samantha jumped, meeting her own guilty gaze in the dresser mirror; she had completely forgotten that Robbie was waiting for her in the living room. "Coming," she called, dropping the newspaper clipping as if it were on fire. Picking up her brush, she whipped it quickly through her heavy fall of hair. "I'm almost ready."

"Yeah, I know what *almost ready* means to you."

"No—" she jerked open her bedroom door, very nearly causing Robbie to fall into the room "—I'm really ready." She linked her arm through the crook of his and steered him toward the front door. "Tell you what, Robbie," she said in a sudden burst of inspiration. "Instead of Angelo's, let's go someplace swanky. My treat. After all, I'm the Sophisticated Lady now." She mugged a little, looking at him over her shoulder in a badly done imitation of some sultry sex symbol. "I should only be seen in the very best places, don't you agree?"

"Sure, if you want to." He shrugged. "Might as well see how the other half lives, I guess."

"Especially since we're one of them now."

"Not me." He pointed an unsteady finger at her. "You."

"Both of us." She held up her hand to forestall the argument she could see coming. "Let's just go eat," she said. "I'm starving."

2

LONDON! She could hardly believe she was finally here. If she weren't so darned tired, Samantha thought, flopping backward onto the hotel bed, she'd change into her jeans and get started on her sight-seeing. She had a whole list of places that she wanted to see—the changing of the guard at Buckingham Palace, the Tower of London, Big Ben, Hyde Park, Westminster Abbey, Trafalgar Square, Harrods Department Store.

"I want to ride the underground," she'd told Robbie as their plane sped over the Atlantic. "And have high tea at one of the hotels on Hyde Park. Cream buns and scones. And those fancy little watercress sandwiches without the crust."

"The underground is just a subway," Robbie had pointed out, "and cream buns will make even you fat."

Leave it to Robbie to be a wet blanket, she thought, staring up at the ceiling of her hotel room as she remembered their conversation. Especially lately. His mood had been decidedly testy ever since he'd signed the contract to take the pictures for the *Sophisticated Lady* campaign.

She knew that his poor attitude stemmed from the fact that he was nervous. Robbie was always nervous at the beginning of a new job, mainly because he was never really sure of himself and his talent. And this was the biggest job he'd ever had.

No matter how much evidence he had to the contrary, and despite the fact that it was his brilliant test shots of her that had gotten them both their current jobs, he seemed to have the feeling that he'd been merely coasting along on luck, or something, and this time the powers that be would finally find him out.

Robbie had always been what Samantha privately thought of as emotionally fragile. He'd even undergone a few sessions with a therapist, back in the days when they first became stepbrother and stepsister, at fourteen and sixteen respectively. Robbie's teenage insecurity had taken the form of periodic rebellion, which eventually included a few brushes with the law for petty shoplifting and other misdemeanor crimes. He was better now, of course. Stronger and more able to cope with the slings and arrows of life, and yet . . .

Samantha sighed. She hadn't seen him quite so edgy and oppressively pessimistic since that long-ago time when he was still feeling insecure in the new family situation. And it was insecurity this time, too. Silly, but that was Robbie. The best thing she could do for him, she knew, was to be as understanding as possible and try not to make him feel any worse than he already did. Unfortunately her own bubbling excitement refused to be contained.

She was being treated like a star by the Gavino Cosmetics staff, and everything—the makeup and wardrobe consultations, the test shots, the conferences with the advertising people, the location shooting at the Trump Tower and the Empire State Building and in

Central Park—was wonderful and exciting. She was having the time of her life, and no matter how she tried to downplay it, it showed.

Even Robbie, she thought, must have realized that it was impossible to expect her not to be wildly enthusiastic about all the wonderful things that were happening in her life. But apparently he didn't. The more she enthused about the *Sophisticated Lady* campaign and the people involved in it, the more morose Robbie became. And he got really sulky whenever Nick Gavino's name cropped up in her conversation. So she tried not to let it.

It wasn't all that hard, actually, because she'd just about managed to convince herself that what she'd felt in Nick Gavino's conference room could be attributed to her quite natural excitement over being chosen as the Sophisticated Lady. And it stood to reason that her excitement and sense of anticipation about the assignment would have bubbled over onto the man responsible. And yet ... And yet she couldn't quite explain—nor entirely forget—the soft laughter they'd shared, or that gleam in his hot-coffee eyes, or that feeling that had held them tense and still for a heartbeat's worth of time.

She sighed again and jumped up from the bed, refusing to spend any more time thinking about it. At least not right now. Right now she was going sightseeing.

According to the Michelin guidebook she dug out of her purse, Hyde Park should be just across the street from the hotel. She could spend a couple of enjoyable hours exploring the park and, since it was so close, she wouldn't have to chance getting lost in the underground. Plus, she thought, there was bound to be a hot dog stand or a crumpet seller or something, somewhere in the park so she could get a snack to tied her over until dinner.

She tossed the guidebook on the bed and kicked off her elegant high-heeled pumps. *Sophisticated Lady* shoes was how she thought of them. They'd been chosen for her by the Gavino Cosmetics people, as had everything else she'd be wearing for the *Sophisticated Lady* campaign. They were all things she might have chosen for herself if she'd had the money and the occasion, not to mention the life-style, to wear them. She grinned at herself in the mirror. Now she had all three, she realized happily. All she had to do was learn how to be comfortable dressed like a sophisticated woman of the world. But not now. Now was the time for jeans.

She dug a pair of skinny black Levi's out of her suitcase and stepped into them, flopping backward onto the bed in order to zip up the fly. Standing upright, she pulled a soft red turtleneck sweater on over her head. Then, tugging her hair free of the collar, she stamped her feet into her black half boots, shrugged into a shiny, black leather bomber jacket and slung a snappy zebra print satchel over her shoulder. She was ready for her first London adventure.

"Robbie." She tapped on the door across the hall from hers. "Robbie, I'm going across to the park. Wanna come?"

She heard the sound of fumbling footsteps, a muffled curse, and then the door swung open. "What?" Robbie said groggily. His hair was messed up and there were rippled impressions across one cheek, as if he'd been sleeping facedown against the bedspread.

He looked sweet and rumpled, Samantha thought, like a little boy just awakened from his nap. All her vague annoyance at him fled. "I'm going across to the park," she said. "Do you want to come with me?"

"Good God, no! I'm bushed." He peered at her through the slits of his half-closed eyes, pushing at the wiry brown curls that fell over his forehead with one hand. "Why aren't you?"

"Why aren't I what?"

"Tired."

Samantha shrugged. "I don't know. Too excited, I guess."

Robbie snorted in disgust. "Figures."

She grinned unrepentantly and turned to go, then checked and glanced back over her shoulder. "See you at dinner?"

"Yeah, I guess." He pushed at his hair again. "Have a good time," he said through a yawn. "And watch those cream buns. No more than half a dozen."

Samantha flashed him another smile before the door closed and then all but skipped down the hall to the elevators. The afternoon sunlight beckoned to her through the revolving doors as she hurried across the quietly opulent lobby of the hotel, oblivious to the admiring stares that followed her tall willowy figure and the shining mass of her hair as it swung against her shoulders.

"Good afternoon, miss," said the uniformed doorman as she stepped out onto the sidewalk.

"Good afternoon." She beamed at him, her wide gray eyes shining like sun-sparkled water. "It's a lovely day, isn't it?" she said, lifting her face to the weak spring sunshine.

"That it is, miss," he agreed. "May I call you a taxi?"

Absently she brushed her wind-tossed hair out of her face. "No, thank you. I'm just going across to the park for a while." She waved a little farewell and stepped off the curb.

A car whizzed by, its horn blaring loudly, just inches in front of her. At the same instant she felt an iron hand clamp on to her upper arm, yanking her back to the pavement. She turned shakily to thank her rescuer, expecting to see the hotel doorman at her side.

Her eyes widened in surprise—and sudden, bubbling excitement. "Mr. Gavino!"

HE'D BEEN SURE that he'd exaggerated his reaction to her that day in the conference room. She was a beautiful woman, yes, but he was used to beautiful women. She was also extraordinarily sexy and elegant but he was used to that, too. If he'd thought of her nearly every day it was only because he'd been forced by business to think about her. Decisions about the *Sophisticated Lady* and, thus, about Samantha Spencer had to be made on a regular and frequent basis at this point in the campaign.

So, when she'd stared up at him from the glossy New York photos spread out over his desk—in a hundred different poses, settings and moods—he told himself that he didn't feel anything but a very natural masculine appreciation for her cool blond beauty and a sense of immense satisfaction that he'd made the right choice for his Sophisticated Lady.

It was something of a jolt to realize that he'd been wrong...or lying to himself. Because here he was, standing on a London sidewalk with his hand curled around her soft upper arm, smelling the faint scent of her flowery perfume drifting to him and feeling his gut tighten with something a lot stronger than mere appreciation for a beautiful woman or satisfaction at a job well done.

What he was feeling, he realized, was desire. Not an unknown emotion by any means, and when he stopped to think about it, not an unreasonable one, either, given the fact that she was exactly the type of woman he preferred. It wasn't even a totally unwelcome emotion, even if she was technically an employee. For two sophisticated, worldly people, mixing business with pleasure shouldn't present any problems at all, *if* he decided to pursue it.

"You have to look both ways," he said, in a low tone. "Traffic moves just the opposite of what you're used to. And my name is Nick."

"Yes, opposite," she echoed softly, her mind running riot. *He's here! In London!* She'd known he was going to drop in on them, of course, to see how things were progressing with his Sophisticated Lady but she hadn't expected to see him so soon. So unexpectedly. It made her heart race and her brain go numb.

Nick frowned. "Are you all right?"

"What?" She blinked like a child just waking up from a nap. "Oh, yes. I'm fine," she lied. Actually she felt as if she'd been hit by a truck. Her eyes were slightly glazed from the impact.

"Are you sure you're all right?"

She eased her arm out of his loose grasp; his holding it made her feel curiously faint. "Yes, I'm fine. Really." She nodded to emphasize her words and the breeze lifted her hair, blowing it across her face. A strand or two stuck to the moistness of her lips. She shook her head to dislodge them just as Nick reached up to brush it back. As one, they froze the instant his fingers touched the corner of her mouth—eyes locked, breath bated, both of them remembering that moment in his conference room.

And then Nick smiled, his mind suddenly made up. He was going to mix business with a little pleasure. A *lot* of pleasure. "Your hair's very soft," he murmured, rubbing the silky strands between his fingers.

"Conditioner," she whispered, still struggling to breathe properly. "I use it every morning."

Nick's smile deepened. "I hope it's ours."

"Yes, of course. It's in my contract."

He smoothed the hair back, tucking it behind her ear. "That's good."

"Yes, isn't it? Well, ah . . ." She hesitated, not knowing what else to say with him standing there, looking at her as if she were a chocolate-covered pastry and he a dieter still ten pounds from his goal weight. *Well, when in doubt rely on good manners,* she thought and stuck out her right hand. It shook a little. "Thank you for saving me, Mr. Gavino," she said briskly. "I'll remember to look both ways next time."

He took her offered hand in his. "Nick," he reiterated.

"Nick," she repeated obediently.

They stared at each other for another long, heated moment.

"Well, thank you, Nick," she managed finally. "I'd hate to have ended up squashed by a taxi on my first day in London." She tried, discreetly, to draw her hand from his but he wouldn't let go.

"I'd hate to have seen you squashed, too," he said. "My whole *Sophisticated Lady* campaign would have been squashed with you. And that would be disastrous, wouldn't it?"

"Yes, it would," Samantha agreed, letting her hand relax in his. She didn't really want it back, anyway.

"We'd have to start all over, trying to find a new Sophisticated Lady." He stroked her knuckles with his thumb as he spoke. "My board wouldn't like that," he murmured, watching her eyes widen and warm under his touch. "They seem to think that I've already spent too much money on this campaign."

"I guess you've invested a lot of money in this campaign, then?" she said inanely, just to have something to say. Her hand, she realized, was tingling.

"Millions," he agreed softly, wondering with a part of his mind just how soon he could get her into his bed. Not long, if her reaction to his hand on hers was any indication.

"Well, I guess I'd better get going." She tried again to withdraw her hand from his.

"Going?" He tightened his hold. She wasn't going anywhere. Not yet. Not without him.

"Sight-seeing," she said. The wind picked up her hair again, blowing it across her face. "I'm going sight-seeing."

"All by yourself?"

"I asked Robbie but he said he'd rather sleep," she said. "And I don't know anyone else in London."

"You know me."

"Yes." Her voice was breathy with anticipation and invitation.

"You wouldn't mind if I invited myself along, then?" *If she minded that was just too bad.*

"No, of course I wouldn't mind." *Was he kidding?* "But I'm only going over to Hyde Park," she warned him.

"So?"

"So I'm sure you've been there before, haven't you?"

"Well?" he said inquiringly.

"You'd probably be bored."

"I doubt it." He lifted his free hand, trailing his fingers over her cheek as he brushed at the wayward strands of her hair. "But if it worries you we could make it lunch instead."

Samantha swallowed. "Lunch?"

"Umm-hmm. I was just on my way into the hotel for a bite to eat when you tried to throw yourself under that taxi." After lunch they could go to his room. Or hers. He didn't care which.

"Lunch would be lovely," she said, feeling light-headed and just a little like a rabbit caught in the headlights of an oncoming car. "But not in the hotel. I want fish and chips."

"Fish and chips." Nick grimaced. "Really?"

Samantha nodded.

"You don't think you'd like, say, a nice slice of rare roast beef instead. Or a fillet of sole? They do a very nice fillet of sole in the hotel dining room."

"Fish and chips," she said decisively. "This is my first time in London and I want fish and chips. *Authentic.* Served with vinegar and—" she waved her free hand through the air "—everything."

"By 'everything' I suppose you mean that you want it wrapped in newspaper?"

"Of course."

"Of course." Nick sighed, seeing his visions of an afternoon of wild sex with his Sophisticated Lady fading away. But surprisingly it was all right. He could wait for her. And he could enjoy her company without sex. For now. "Well, come on then," he said, resigned. "I know this little Greek place." He turned toward the street to hail a cab.

Samantha tugged at his hand.

"What?"

"Let's walk. It's a gorgeous day."

Nick shook his head. "Too far for walking."

"Well, then, one of the double-deckers?" She grasped his forearm, her face turned up to his, and fluttered her lashes in blatant, exaggerated entreaty. "Please?"

Nick laughed. "Okay, a double-decker it is. Come on." He tightened his hand on hers and they ran for the big red bus that was just beginning to pull away from the curb. Lifting her by the waist, he hoisted her up onto the first step and then swung himself up after her.

"I assume you want to sit on top?" he said with an air of amused indulgence.

"Yes, please." She settled down on to the hard bench seat. Nick slid in next to her and began pointing out the sights like a professional tour guide.

His shoulder touched hers each time he leaned over her to point out yet another landmark, filling her with a tingling warmth. His after-shave, a faint woodsy scent with undertones of musk, filled her nostrils. His breath, smelling faintly of peppermint and brandy, was warm on her cheek. And his voice, as deep and melodic as a sorcerer's song, filled her ears. Her mind wandered from the London sights she should have been savoring—savoring instead the rock-hard thigh brushing against hers.

"This next one is our stop," he said in her ear, fully aware of the effect he was having on her. It was all part of the game: advance and retreat, thrust and parry. He enjoyed it—as long as it stayed a game—and he was good at it.

And so was she, he realized when she slowly lifted her gaze from his thigh, up his hard torso and wide chest to rest finally on his face. "I'm sorry. What did you say?" she murmured, completely unaware that *he* was aware of the leisurely journey her eyes had just taken.

"Our stop," he repeated hoarsely, taking her hand in his. "This is where we get off."

They hurried down the narrow stairs of the bus, their feet clamoring on the metal steps, and tumbled out onto the sidewalk, both of them suddenly breathless and laughing at nothing in particular.

"Smell it?" he asked, an avid expression in his eyes as he watched her.

Samantha cocked her head and sniffed the air like a hunting dog. "Coffee?"

Nick nodded.

"Strong coffee and—" she sniffed again "—frying fish." She pointed down a side street. "That way."

"Lead on," he invited, delighted with her unaffected exuberance.

Laughing, Samantha pulled him along behind her, following her nose to the open door of a tiny restaurant. It was noisy with loud Greek music and voices, redolent with the tantalizing smell of frying fish and crisp golden potatoes. Nick ordered for them both.

"In newspaper," he said to the smiling man behind the counter, even though they were eating inside. "The beautiful lady is a crazy American and she wants her fish and chips in newspaper." Nick tapped his forehead significantly and the Greek laughed, showing the flash of gold in a front tooth. He waved them toward the back of the narrow café, saying he would bring their food to them when it was ready.

"This is nice," observed Samantha, shrugging out of her bomber jacket as they sat down across from each other.

"Yes, very nice," said Nick, his eyes intent as he watched her slip the jacket off her shoulders.

Samantha flushed a bit, the warmth of his gaze making her nipples pucker visibly beneath the soft fabric of her red sweater and the sheer material of her red bra. "I must admit, though," she went on, resolutely ignoring her physical reactions—and his reaction to them, "I expected a Cockney accent behind a fish and chips counter, not Greek."

"Best restaurants in London are Greek." He leaned back to allow the waiter to place the newspaper-wrapped meals in front of them. "Or Indian. Or Chinese."

"No blood pudding?" Her eyes twinkled at him across the width of the table. "No steak and kidney pie? No bangers and mash?"

"Only if you insist." He shook his head and grinned roguishly, looking suddenly young and carefree and sexier than ever. The effect was devastating, Samantha thought. Utterly devastating. "Would you like some coffee to go with that?" he asked.

Samantha shook her head.

"A Coke?"

She wrinkled her nose. "Bite your tongue! A Coke! I can get a Coke in New York."

"Okay, you asked for it." He glanced up at the waiter. "A shandy for the crazy American lady."

"What is it?" she asked suspiciously when the tall glass was placed in front of her.

"Taste it."

Samantha took a cautious sip, and another. Then she smiled and took a big gulp, showing every evidence of real enjoyment.

"You actually like it?" Nick was incredulous.

Samantha leaned across the table. "It's awful!" she confided in a stage whisper, making Nick laugh out loud. "What is it?"

"Beer and lemonade."

"Ugh! No wonder."

"Shall I order you that Coke now?"

"No. If the English drink shandys, then so can I."

"Most of the English very sensibly drink Coke just like everyone else in the world."

Samantha made a face at him and took another determined sip. "Maybe it grows on you," she said hopefully, setting it aside to open her paper-wrapped lunch. Clouds of fragrant steam rose up from the table as she did so. "Okay, how do I do this?" She picked up the bottle of vinegar. "You're the fish and chips expert."

"Just sprinkle it on as if it were salt," Nick instructed her. "Not too much, though. You don't want to make it soggy."

"Delicious," Samantha pronounced, tasting her vinegar-spiced food. "Different but delicious."

"You really enjoy your food, don't you?" he commented, wondering if she indulged her other appetites as freely.

"Mmm-hmm. Awful, isn't it? Robbie says I'm a human garbage disposal." She popped a golden fried chip into her mouth. "I have a weird metabolism, I guess. Never gain any weight."

"Thank God for that. I don't fancy seeing my Sophisticated Lady as a blimp."

"Never happen," she assured him. "In fact, I have to be careful not to lose weight. Really," she added at his skeptical look. "All the other models hate me because I scarf up Big Macs and fries while they have to nibble on rabbit food."

Nick ordered baklava for them both when the fish and chips had been cleared away, and Samantha opted for a cup of the strong Greek coffee, after all, instead of another of the bitter shandys.

"Coffee goes better with the pastry," she defended herself primly when he cocked a teasing eyebrow at her. "Can we get another one to go?" she said a moment later, licking the last of the sticky honey and nut confection from her fingers.

"Your contract's null and void if you get fat," he warned, handing the pastry to her as they left the café.

Samantha just grinned and bit into her second square of baklava.

"Oh, let's walk back to the hotel," she urged a minute later, halting in her tracks as Nick automatically headed for the bus stop. "It's not *that* far." She fluttered her lashes. "Please?"

Once again Nick laughed and gave in. "But don't blame me if your feet hurt tomorrow," he warned, taking her hand in his.

They began to weave their way through the crowd on the busy London street. Ambling in the general direction of the hotel, they stopped every ten minutes or so for Samantha to look into shop windows, unashamedly gawking like the tourist she was. She dragged him, uncomplaining, into an Indian boutique to look at the beautiful saris on display, and ended up buying a little earthenware pot of smoky kohl for her eyes. Their next stop was a china shop where Samantha bought a delicate ceramic cat for her mother. And finally she led him into a woolen outlet, where she decided the sweaters were no less expensive than the ones she could buy at home.

"Harrods next," she said, flipping up the collar on her leather jacket as they exited the woolens store. The sunny spring day had become cloudy, and the breeze had turned into a skirt-tugging wind.

"Cold?" Nick dropped a long arm over her shoulders, pulling her close to his side.

She looked up at him from under her lashes and smiled. "Not anymore," she assured him, wrapping her arm around the hardness of his waist as casually as if she'd done it a hundred times before. Her fingers clutched the fine worsted material of his suit jacket; her shoulder fit perfectly under the curve of his arm; the side of her breast pressed against his hard torso. "I want to see Harrods next," she said again.

"Planning to buy out the store?" he asked a moment later, a note of amusement in his voice as he watched her gaze about the world-famous department store.

"Not this time. I just want to look." She glanced up at him again as she spoke and was struck anew by the impact of his dark good looks. His hot-coffee eyes were full of amused male indulgence. The angle of his lean, shadowed jaw was sharp and clean. The tanned column of his neck was firm and corded with muscle.

"My mother says Harrods is the eighth wonder of the world," she said in an effort to distract her mind with something other than his irresistible appeal. "And, of course—" her voice dropped an octave and took on a clipped New England accent "—Princess Diana shops here, you know. Oh, Nick, look!" Her voice rose again to its customary enthusiastic level. "Isn't that marvelous. It looks too pretty to be real, doesn't it?"

They had entered Harrods Fruit Hall with its mounds of picture-perfect fruit imported from around the world and artistically arranged to tempt the buyer. Firm rosy apples, fuzzy little brown kiwis, some of them sliced open to show the bright green pulp on the inside, pyramids of lemons and oranges, grapefruits and pineapple, rich yellow papayas, ripe cantaloupes and honeydew; they all scented the air of the Fruit Hall.

"I've got to have some of those peaches," she said, inhaling the sweet heady fragrances that swirled around her. "But I, uh, haven't got any English money."

"You just ate," Nick reminded her, but he made the purchase anyway. "Now these are for your breakfast," he said sternly, handing her the small bag of fruit.

"Midnight snack," she countered laughingly, slipping it into the shopping bag that held her other purchases.

Nick shrugged in comic defeat and reached out, drawing her back to his side. Samantha snuggled against him as naturally as breathing, and they continued on their leisurely way through the store, carefully exploring all the food halls.

"Reconnaissance," Nick accused, but Samantha ignored him.

She was fascinated by the displays. Nothing she'd ever seen in New York compared with the lavishness of the food halls at Harrods. The Fresh Meat and Game Hall had all of the usual meats—beef and pork and chicken—but there was quail, too, and pheasant, rabbit and venison.

"As if anyone would want to eat Bambi," she whispered to Nick as they left meats and entered seafoods.

The white-aproned fishmonger offered her a cracker topped with a paper-thin slice of delicate pink salmon when she paused to admire his display. "From Scotland," he informed her proudly, beaming when she bit eagerly into it.

"How come I didn't get one?" Nick whispered against her ear as they moved away.

"Because you don't look hungry?"

The same thing happened in the Dairy Hall, where she was given a thin slice of fresh goat cheese to sample.

"Somebody's told them the way to your heart," Nick groused.

"Through my stomach, you mean?" Samantha considered that briefly. "You're probably right," she agreed.

His lips were very close to her ear. "I hope not."

She halted in the aisle and looked up at him. "Why?"

"Because I can't cook," he said, deadpan.

"Well—" her smile widened flirtatiously "—I don't eat *all* the time."

In that moment, in the space of a heartbeat, they both forgot where they were. Nick's arm shifted on her shoulders, tightening his hold, and he moved so that she was held in front of him instead of at his side. Samantha lifted her face until her eyes were on a level with his mouth.

"Nick," she said invitingly, unaware that she'd whispered his name.

His dark head bent, descending toward her parted lips, and Samantha came up on her tiptoes, eager to meet him halfway. But the kiss didn't happen. Someone jostled them from behind—a fellow shopper who hadn't sidestepped their immobile figures quickly enough—and the fragile mood was shattered. Nick swore softly and lifted his head. Samantha sighed and sank back on her heels.

"We'd better get back to the hotel," he said gruffly, turning her in his embrace. "It's getting late." They turned together toward the nearest exit.

It was later than either of them had realized. The grayness of dusk had fallen while they were inside, and the street was full of shoppers and workers hurrying home after the day's industry. Samantha zipped up her jacket, snuggling under Nick's sheltering arm as they hurried along the busy sidewalk in the direction of the hotel, heads down against the now brisk wind.

"Six," she told him when they entered the elevator. Nick pushed the appropriate button and they rode up to her floor, oddly silent after all of the easy playful conversation that had carried them through the afternoon. Both of them were thinking of that interrupted kiss, wondering if it would happen now, wondering where it would lead if it did.

"Your key," he said, holding out his hand when they stopped in front of her door.

"I had a wonderful afternoon, Nick," she said to his back as he fitted the key in the lock. "The fish and chips were great. And even the shandy wasn't so bad once I got used to it." She was babbling, she knew, as suddenly unaccountably nervous as a teenager on her first date. "You were very patient with all my shopping and—" Her voice trailed off as he pushed open the door to her hotel room and turned toward her.

Now was the moment, she thought. If he was going to kiss her it would be now. He put his hands on her shoulders, pulling her to him. She lifted her face, not bothering to hide her eagerness.

"I had a wonderful afternoon, too," he said softly, meaning it. If it ended now, it would still be a wonderful afternoon. *But I'd rather it didn't end now*, he thought, and then his head bent and he touched his mouth to hers.

He kissed her lightly at first, lips barely touching, tongue held back, waiting until she indicated her readiness for more. If seduction were a game, then Nick was a master, never pushing for more than his partner was ready to give, always knowing the right moment to press his suit. And then Samantha parted her lips under his and he forgot all about games.

He angled his head on instinct alone, opening his mouth over hers as he accepted her invitation to taste the sweetness inside. His arms came around her pliant body, hugging her slender back. His body pressed against hers, hungry and eager and hard.

Samantha leaned into him, a handful of his suit jacket in one hand, her shopping bag dangling from the other. She felt as if her skin was burning and her bones were melting and her blood was bubbling in her veins. When Nick finally lifted his head—much, much too soon—they were both gasping for air.

"I don't suppose you'd consider asking me in?" he said raggedly, his forehead resting against hers.

For just a moment, for just a mindless, reckless, wonderfully heedless moment, Samantha considered it. It would be heavenly, she knew. Beyond anything she had ever experienced if this one kiss was anything to judge by. And she knew, instinctively, that it was. "No,

I don't think so," she whispered, shaking her head with real regret.

"Never?" he whispered, disappointment evident in his deep voice.

No, not never. "Well, I, ah . . ."

He sighed and straightened, reaching to grasp the hand still clutching his jacket. He lifted it, cupping it in his. "It's too soon for you." He dropped her room key into her palm and folded her trembling fingers over it. And then he reached up and tilted her chin with his forefinger. "But I'll ask again," he said seriously. "Soon." His hot-coffee eyes wandered over her face. His thumb brushed across her moist, parted lips. "Very soon."

Samantha just nodded, too dazed to speak.

"I'll meet you in the cocktail lounge at eight," he said. "Then we'll go out to dinner with the rest of the crew. Okay?"

Samantha nodded again.

Nick bent his head and brushed his lips over hers once more. And a second time, for just a fraction of a second longer. And then he turned on his heel and headed down the hall to the elevators before his good intentions gave way to his baser instincts and he did what his clamoring body—and her wide, unguarded eyes—were urging him to do.

3

SAMANTHA SAGGED against the doorjamb, her dazed eyes devouring the rigid set of his back as he retreated down the hall. She watched him as he stabbed the elevator button, as he stood there, waiting for the elevator. Then the doors slid open and he stepped inside and was gone. Samantha felt as if she'd been deserted.

"Oh, don't be such a dope," she said aloud, rousing herself enough to get inside her hotel room. "You're the one who sent him away." She closed the door and leaned back against it, a dreamy little smile on her face, her hands unconsciously cradling the shopping bag to her chest.

"I'll ask again," he'd said. *"Soon."*

How soon was soon?

Tonight? Tomorrow night? She pushed away from the door with a sigh and dropped her shopping bag and her zebra-striped satchel on the bed. Tonight, tomorrow night, the time really didn't matter all that much because, whenever he asked, however soon *soon* was, she knew her answer would very likely be yes. Especially if he kissed her again when he did his asking.

"You shameless hussy, you." She grinned at herself in the full-length mirror attached to the closet door. "What would Mother say?"

She knew exactly what her mother would say. "Really, Samantha, dear." She could almost hear Margaret Spencer's clipped New England accent. "Are you being quite wise?"

No, she thought, *probably not*.

After all, she reminded herself, she didn't really know anything about him. Oh, sure, she knew that he was rich and good-looking and still unmarried at thirty-four, that he gave generously to a number of charities, that he had turned a small family-owned company into a thriving international conglomerate in less than fifteen years. Anybody who read the newspapers knew that much about him.

But somehow it just didn't seem to matter.

What mattered was that he had a wonderfully warm laugh that made her want to laugh with him. And that his eyes heated when he looked at her, causing her blood to heat in response. And that his kiss moved her more than anything ever had in her life before.

But maybe a little caution was called for, anyway. Because without it, she just might be setting herself up for a fall by letting things move *too* quickly with a man of Nick Gavino's obvious experience.

She stared at her reflection in the mirror, trying to think it through objectively. Her face, she noted, was flushed. Her eyes were sparkling. And her lips kept wanting to turn up in an idiot's smile of pure delight. Forget objectivity, she thought. There was no way she could be objective about Nick Gavino. There was no way she wanted to be. Besides, she assured herself, things weren't moving all *that* quickly, anyway; she'd been thinking about Nick ever since that day in the conference room. Wondering about him at odd moments. Wanting to know small inconsequential things. Did he prefer tea or coffee in the morning? What was his favorite color? What kind of pet did he have as a little boy?

I must be falling in love, she thought, shaking her head at herself.

Love would certainly explain the empty, fluttering feeling in her stomach and the faint sense of lightheadedness she'd been feeling ever since she'd bumped into him in front of the hotel.

Or, maybe, I'm just hungry again.

She turned from the mirror and headed for the bathroom. Eight o'clock wasn't that far away and she had lots to do to get ready.

SAMANTHA HAD TAKEN her bath and done her makeup and was putting the finishing touches on her crimped hair when Robbie pounded on her hotel door. "Room service," he hollered.

"Just a minute." She tightened the sash of her robe and flipped the dead bolt. "Come on in," she invited, holding the door wide as Robbie strolled past her into the middle of the room. "My, don't you look nice."

He was dressed in a pair of loose, pleated-front tan slacks, an oatmeal jacket in a heavy linen-look fabric, and a striped button-down shirt in shades of peach and cream.

"Very nice," she said again. "I don't think I've ever seen you look quite so spiffy before."

He fingered the knot of his knubby-textured cocoa-brown tie. "Is this tied right?"

"Take your hand away and let me see." Samantha tweaked the knot. "Perfect," she said, leaning forward to give him a quick, sisterly peck of approval.

He put his hands on her shoulders, holding her. "So do you. Almost," he said teasingly. "So you'd better get a move on. It's a quarter to already and Gavino—" he drawled the name, sounding somehow disdainful as he said it "—left orders for us to meet him in the cocktail lounge at eight sharp."

"It's *Mr.* Gavino," she reprimanded him automatically. "Or Nick."

"Since when did he become Nick?"

"Since the contract-signing party. He asked me—us—to call him Nick, remember?"

"Yeah, I remember."

"I've got to finish getting ready," Samantha said then, moving out from under his hands. "Do you want to wait for me here or downstairs?"

"Here." Robbie flipped on the television and sat down on the foot of the bed to watch it.

Samantha got her dress out of the closet and her shoes out of her suitcase and went back into the bathroom to change. After drawing on a pair of sheer, French-cut panty hose, she slipped the dress from its hanger and stepped into it. Black and bare, it was made of bias-cut silk to lovingly hug every slender curve of her body from bust to knee. The bodice was low and scooped, showing the uppermost curve of her small, high breasts. Shoestring straps studded with rhine-stones secured it over her shoulders, criss-crossing over her bare back. Her heels were high and black, too, with tiny rhinestone buckles that fastened around her slim ankles.

She inserted glitzy rhinestone and faux emerald earrings into her pierced ears, fluffed her crimped hair so that it floated, full and wavy, around her face and stepped back to assess her mirrored image.

On a more voluptuous woman the dress would have come across as highly suggestive, but on her tall, model-thin frame it looked only subtly sexy, elegantly sophisticated and even quite ladylike. Amazing what being a tad too skinny let you get away with as far as clothes were concerned, she thought, searching through the *Sophisticated Lady* cosmetics spread on the counter over the sink. Finding what she needed, she dusted a little blusher along her collarbones and the tops of her shoulders and the exposed curve of her breasts, then stepped back again, her head tilted as she considered the effect.

Too bad I don't look this good in my birthday suit, she thought, pleased with what she'd achieved. The phone rang, interrupting her narcissistic wanderings.

"Grab that for me, will you, Robbie?" she called from the bathroom. "I'll be out in a minute." She sprayed a cloud of Gavino Cosmetics' *Night Magic* cologne into the air and walked through it as she left the bathroom.

Robbie was just hanging up the phone. She glanced over at him as she crossed to the closet for her coat.

"Who was it?" she asked, slipping into a heavy black satin evening coat. It had a high mandarin collar, long narrow sleeves and was lined in shimmering emerald green. "Robbie?" she said again, turning to him as she lifted her hair out of the collar.

He had a strange look on his face.

"Robbie?" Images of accidents back home leaped to mind. She reached out, putting a hand on his arm. "What is it?"

"Did you enjoy Hyde Park this afternoon?"

Her hand dropped. So that was it. "That was Nick, I take it?"

Robbie nodded.

"Then you already know that I didn't go to Hyde Park this afternoon, obviously, or you wouldn't have asked." She smiled. "But the afternoon was just lovely anyway. We went to this little Greek place that Nick knows, for fish and chips."

"I told you he was after you."

"Oh, Robbie, really. Let's not start that again," she said, exasperation and fondness mixed in her voice. Robbie had always been protective of her, attempting to vet her boyfriends as if he were her older brother. This was just more of the same and she handled it the way she had always handled it. "It's nice of you to worry about me," she said, flipping open her slender evening bag to make sure she had her key. "But I'm a big girl now." She closed the bag with a snap and tucked it under her arm. "All set," she announced, heading for the door.

"Maybe you want him to be after you," Robbie accused her.

Samantha looked back over her shoulder. He hadn't moved from the telephone stand beside the bed. "Yes," she said. "Maybe I do." And *that*, she thought, could certainly qualify as the understatement of the year. "Now, shall we go?"

"He's a shark." Robbie came forward to put his hand on her shoulder. "Trust me, Sammie. I know his type."

"Oh, really?" She moved out from under his hand to the hallway. "And just how many drop-dead handsome, millionaire business tycoons do you know?"

"Is that it? You're interested in his money?"

The door clicked shut with a definite snap. "I like his body, too," Samantha said pleasantly but her back was stiff with growing anger as she headed down the hall to the elevators.

"Hey, I didn't mean it like that, Sammie," Robbie said anxiously, hurrying to catch up with her. "I just—" He shrugged, reaching out to punch the elevator call button.

"You just what?" Samantha said, slanting him a sideways look.

"I just...care about you, that's all." They stepped into the elevator. "And I don't want to see you hurt by this Gavino character. He's the kind of guy who collects beautiful women like trophies. He doesn't care about what's on the inside," Robbie said seriously. "And you're so trusting. He'll break your heart if you let him, Sammie." He put his hand on her shoulder again, squeezing it when she didn't shake him off. "I don't want to see that happen."

Samantha's annoyance melted at his sincere concern. "It won't happen, Robbie." She reached up and patted the hand on her shoulder. "I promise," she said as the elevator came to a stop.

Nick was standing a few feet away from the bank of elevators, scowling at his watch. He looked up as the doors slid open, a smile smoothing out the impatient crease between his eyes when he saw her.

Samantha felt her heart give a little lurch at the sight of him. *I am falling in love*, she thought. And then she was hurrying forward, slipping out from under Robbie's hand as she held her own toward the dark-eyed man who extended his to her.

Nick felt his pulse quicken. His reaction wasn't just to her incredible beauty, he told himself, although that was part of it. It had more to do with the warmth of her smile and the uncensored look of pleasure that widened her eyes when she caught sight of him, the eager way she reached for his hand without coyness. He appreciated a woman who could indicate her interest in a man without the need for declarations of love and commitment.

"I'm sorry I'm late," she said a bit breathlessly, smiling up at him. "Turning into the Sophisticated Lady by myself took a little longer than I expected."

Nick took her other hand, looking her over as leisurely as if there were no one else around. The fragile heels she wore made her already impossibly long legs look even longer. The rather severe black satin coat enhanced her natural elegance. And whatever she'd done to her hair caused it to ripple around her face and shoulders like a silvery cloud, giving her a look of fey, fairytale-princess seductiveness that was excitingly at odds with her otherwise up-to-the-minute sophistication.

"The wait was worth it," he said, caressing her with his voice as he had just done with his eyes. "You look lovely." His hands tightened fractionally on hers. "And extremely elegant."

"So do you," she said softly, still smiling up at him from under the sweep of her lashes.

And he did. He looked terribly elegant. His custom-tailored suit was black. His tie was a gray, black and red paisley silk. His shirt was silky white cotton batiste, which looked even more snowy-white against the exciting darkness of his complexion. With the red silk pocket square peeking out of his breast pocket, the discreet gold collar pin just showing under the knot of his tie, and the pair of small, beautifully worked gold cuff links winking from his shirt sleeves, he could have graced the cover of a *Gentlemen's Quarterly* issue on power dressing.

Very elegant, indeed. And very masculine. Very desirable. He made every other man in the lobby seem like a mere boy, Samantha thought, unconsciously eating him with her eyes.

"Are we having dinner in the hotel?" Robbie said in a peeved voice, reminding them that there were other people present.

It was all Nick could do to tear his eyes away from Samantha's enthralled—and enthralling—gaze. "Just drinks," he said, pleasantly enough, despite the heat building up inside him. He forced himself to let go of Samantha's hand, holding his own out to the younger man.

Robbie had no choice but to take it.

"Good to see you again," Nick said, but his eyes had already wandered back to Samantha's face. "Everyone else is in the cocktail lounge," he told her, tucking her hand into the crook of his arm. "This way."

Everyone else turned out to be other members of the *Sophisticated Lady* crew. Samantha already knew the production manager, Terri Gunnerson, and Taylor Jones, the male model, from having worked with them in New York, but the others were English.

Jeffrey Wainwright, a rugged-looking cowboy type with an upper crust English accent would be doing her hair. The makeup artist, a typical English rose except for the streak of lavender in her short blond hair, went by the name of Lulu.

"That's all, luv," she said when she was introduced to Samantha. "Just Lulu."

The rest of the group—two men in business suits and a woman in a floppy bow tie and well-bred tweeds— were Gavino Industries' executives of some sort, here merely to meet the Sophisticated Lady.

"What would you like?" Nick asked, sliding Samantha's chair in behind her as he spoke.

You. The thought came, unbidden, as she tilted her head back to look at him. The movement exposed the long line of her throat and the slight but enticing swell of her cleavage between the open lapels of her satin coat. Her hair touched his hands where they rested on the back of her chair. It felt like liquid moonlight—soft and cool and weightless as it brushed his skin.

"To drink," he said gruffly when she continued to stare at him. "What would you like to drink?"

"Oh." Samantha straightened, looking down at her lap as Nick settled into the seat beside her. "I'll have a—" She looked up at him as his arm slid along the back of her chair. Her breath caught in her throat. He was so close.

"A shandy?" he asked, leaning closer. His tone was low, his expression conspiratorial and intimate and teasing.

Samantha shook her head, her eyes never leaving his. "No, thank you."

"A glass of white wine, then?" he suggested. Her hair was touching his hand again and the heady scents of jasmine, tea roses and musk filled his nostrils, intensified and warmed by the heat of her body. He wondered where she applied it. Behind her ears? On the side of her neck? Between her breasts? On the backs of her knees?

"No, nothing. I—" Samantha licked her lips and looked away, disconcerted by the fact that she could almost *feel* him touching her with his eyes—her ears, her neck, her breasts . . . She felt her nipples swell and pucker and was grateful for the concealing fabric of her satin evening coat. Without it, the aroused state of her body would be visible beneath the fine silk of her elegant dress.

Not that she begrudged Nick the sight. Not at all. She had a sudden, fierce, almost overwhelming desire for him to know exactly how he affected her—and to see for herself how she affected him.

"Nick, I—"

"Do we have time for another round, Nick, old man?" asked someone from across the table.

It took every ounce of willpower he possessed for Nick to answer the man civilly. "Better not," he said after a quick glance at his watch. "I've made reservations for nine." He signaled for the cocktail waitress to bring him the check and rose to his feet, starting the exodus toward the hotel lobby.

The restaurant Nick took them to was Italian, but, the white-coated waiter informed them, they also served steaks and a few typically English specialities as well.

"Blood pudding?" Nick said, a gleam in his eye as he glanced at Samantha.

"Unfortunately, no, sir," the waiter said, thinking the question had been meant for him. "But we do serve a very nice Yorkshire pudding with our roast beef." He looked slightly puzzled when Samantha laughed and shook her head.

"Italian, please." She handed the tasseled menu back to the waiter. "You order for me," she said to Nick, reaching out to touch the back of his hand lightly. The fine black hairs were as soft as they looked. His skin was warm. "You did such a good job this afternoon," she complimented him teasingly, unaware that she had made it sound as if there had been more than the ordering of lunch between them.

No one seemed to notice her unintentional double entendre except Robbie. But Samantha was still smiling up at Nick and didn't see her stepbrother's frown deepen.

"Yes, order for me, too, Nick," chimed in Lulu. "I don't recognize anything on this menu except spaghetti with meat sauce." She waved the menu at the approaching waiter. "Here you go, luv," she said, handing it to him with a smile.

"Great idea," said one of the businessmen, second-ing the motion. "Nick can order for all of us. I'm sure he knows more about Italian food than the rest of us put together," he added, referring to his employer's ethnic background.

Nick looked around the table. "Any objections?"

It seemed for a minute that Robbie was going to ob-ject. And not with a simple, "I'd prefer to order my own meal, thanks." His light hazel eyes blazed across the ta-ble at Samantha for a long, charged second and then flickered challengingly to Nick, for all the world like a bulldog guarding a bone.

What is the matter with him? Samantha wondered.

She appreciated his concern for her but he was tak-ing his big brother routine entirely too far. She was about to tell him so, too, but Nick touched her hand with his and shook his head.

Not now, his look said and Samantha subsided, let-ting it lie. But Robbie wasn't content to leave it at that.

"I guess I haven't got much choice," he growled, practically shoving the menu into the waiter's hands. "It's your money."

Every head turned toward him and it seemed, for just a second, as if they were holding their collective breath, waiting for Nick's wrath to fall. But nothing hap-pened. Nick simply looked at Robbie for a second more, a flash of something very like pity, or perhaps contempt, in his dark eyes. And then, very deliber-ately, he turned his attention to the menu and the waiter, who was hovering attentively at his elbow.

4

"YOU ALL GO AHEAD," Nick said, putting his hand on Samantha's arm as everyone began piling into the two taxis that had pulled up to the curb outside the restaurant. He raised his free hand to hail a third one. "The Sophisticated Lady and I are going for a quick spin around Hyde Park—" he slanted a teasing glance at Samantha "—since she didn't get a chance to see it this afternoon."

Robbie stopped short, half-in, half-out of the taxi. "Do you think you ought to, Sammie?" he said, frowning as he turned around to face them. "You know how hard it is for you to get up in the morning." He looked at Nick, his voice and manner confidingly man-to-man. "She can be a real bear when she first wakes up," he said, making it sound as if they shared more than their first cup of coffee every morning.

Samantha's jaw dropped at the implication in his words.

"And she looks like a hag in front of the camera if she doesn't get enough sleep," he went on before she could say anything.

Samantha took a half step forward. *Damn it, Robbie, that's enough,* her eyes said.

Nick's hand tightened on her arm, stilling her intended outburst. "Impossible." He settled her satin coat on her shoulders, holding it there with his cupped hands. "I'm sure Samantha could never look anything but stunning. But to ease your mind—" a small, very male smile curved his mouth as his eyes met Robbie's over her head "—I promise to have her tucked into bed before midnight."

So there! thought Samantha, sending Robbie a glare before she allowed Nick to turn her toward the third taxi.

"I wouldn't be too hard on him if I were you," Nick advised wryly as they settled into the back seat.

"Too hard on him! I'd like to wring his neck! How could he imply that . . . that . . ." she sputtered, unable to put it into words. The thought of anything more than sibling affection between her and Robbie was too ridiculous to contemplate. Robbie was her *brother*, and for him to pretend otherwise out of some misguided sense of protectiveness would have been laughable if it wasn't so enraging—and embarrassing. Still, he meant it for the best. Hopefully. She sighed. "He's not usually so hard to get along with," she ventured.

Nick glanced at her skeptically.

"No, really, he isn't. Most of the time he's just a nice, normal guy," she said, wondering why she was even bothering to defend him. The way he'd been acting lately, he didn't deserve her loyalty, and yet . . .

Old memories, uneasy recollections of other times prodded at her conscience. When he acted like this he didn't deserve her loyalty, but he needed it. She turned slightly, putting a hand on Nick's sleeve in a gesture that asked for understanding for her temperamental stepbrother. "It's just that something—" *this job* "—has been bothering him lately and it makes him act a little strange."

Nick lifted her hand from his sleeve and turned it over in both of his, gazing down at it as if he were a fortune teller. Her palm was faintly pink, her fingers long and elegant, her nails short and simply manicured. He wondered again what they'd feel like on his body. "You're what's bothering him," he said without looking at her.

"Me?"

"The poor fool's in love with you."

"Oh, no, Nick, you're wrong. We've never—" She broke off, flustered as he touched one finger to the center of her palm. "I mean, well, despite what he tried to make you think, there's never been anything like that between us."

"You don't have to justify your past to me, Samantha," he said, stroking her palm lightly. Her past—any woman's past—was of no interest to him, any more than their future was in any personal sense, once an affair was over. And that's all he ever had—affairs. Anything else was too dangerous. Still, some part of him was glad, very glad, to know that Robbie had never been her lover.

"I mean, he loves me, yes," she went on, intent that there be no misunderstanding. "And I love him. But it's, uh..." Nick's fingers were on her wrist now, following the delicate blue veins up the inside of her arm. "But I love him like a brother. And he, uh—" she swallowed as Nick lifted her palm to his lips "—he loves me like a sister." He flicked the inside of her wrist with his tongue, tasting the tiny pulse that beat there. It was the most exquisite, most tantalizing caress she'd ever known. "That's all, really," she said faintly, staring at the top of his bent head.

"Ah, Samantha." He looked up, capturing her eyes with his. "Lovely Samantha. So sophisticated, yet so naive." He reached out and touched her cheek, lightly brushing the silvery, moon-kissed hair back from her face. "No man with red blood in his veins who isn't your brother is going to love you like a brother. It would be impossible."

"But he *is* my brother. Or, stepbrother, actually. His mother married my father when..." Her voice, already a mere whisper, faded away completely as Nick bent his head again to trail his lips slowly up the inside of her forearm to the sensitive crook of her elbow.

She'd read about this happening, had seen it in old Charles Boyer movies, but she never expected to have it happen to her. Modern men just didn't do this sort of thing. She sat very still, her heart hammering, afraid that the slightest movement on her part might cause him to stop.

His lips reached her shoulder. He nudged her coat aside with his cheek and she felt his warm breath caress the vulnerable curve of her neck. His hands settled on her bare upper arms, holding her for his nuzzling kisses. She sighed, squirming deliciously when his lashes tickled her, and arched her neck sideways to give him better access. The cab swayed as the driver steered around an obstruction in the road. Their bodies swayed, too, sliding along the smooth upholstery, farther into a corner of the cab. Nick never even looked up.

"Nick." She touched his cheek lightly with one hand. "Nick." Surely the driver could see everything that was going on.

Nick lifted his head, drawing back just enough to look at her. His eyes were hot and wanting, barely controlled. His lips were so close that she could almost taste the sweetness of his kiss.

Samantha forgot all about what the taxi driver might see between one breath and the next. Her fingers, seemingly of their own accord, drifted from his lean cheek to stroke through the dark, shiny hair at his temple. Delicately, her touch feather-light, she urged him forward. "Kiss me, Nick," she whispered.

Nick's hot-coffee eyes blazed like wildfire and his hands slid from her arms to her back, dislodging the satin coat as he pulled her pliant body close and touched his lips to hers.

Samantha sighed and shivered, giving herself up to the pleasure of it. She stroked him softly, wonderingly, one hand tangled in the thickness of his hair, the other caressing the hard batiste-covered wall of his chest as it lifted and fell beneath her palm. She could feel the heat of him through his silky shirt, smell the faint scent of his musky after-shave, taste the heady sweetness of the anise-flavored Sambuca that had ended their meal.

Her hand at the back of his head urged him closer, wanting more of him, offering more of herself. Nick turned her a little, pressing her back against the seat as he angled his head to deepen their kiss. Samantha's mouth opened wider under his, eagerly accepting the thrust of his seeking tongue, using her own to taste the hot sweetness he offered her.

His hands moved on her body, then, gently knead-
ing the smooth flesh of her bare back, and she felt the
heel of one hand press against the outside curve of her
breast. She moved restlessly, instinctively seeking further, fuller contact. He moved his hand again, sliding
over the black silk of her dress, and covered one yearning breast.

Samantha moaned softly.

"God, you're delicious," Nick breathed raggedly,
drawing away to kiss her cheeks and chin and eyelids
while his palm cupped her breast. The heat of his hand
seared her through the thin fabric. "I've wanted this for
days. No, weeks," he admitted. "Ever since that day in
my conference room when you touched me—" he
reached up for the hand in his hair "—here," he said,
pressing her fingertips to the corner of his mouth. "I've
dreamed about your hands all over me." His thumb
brushed lightly, back and forth, across her nipple. "My
hands on you."

Heat and longing skittered along her nerve endings.
"Nick." Her fingertips traced his upper lip feverishly but
delicately, like a blind person trying to see through her
sense of touch. "Nick," she repeated, unable to say
anything else with her blood racing through her veins
and her heart pounding in her ears and her bones li-
quifying.

But he knew what she wanted. He pulled her hand
away from his mouth, dragging it down to his lap, and
covered her lips with his. His kiss was deep, seductive,
skillful. His tongue plundered her open mouth. His
palm caressed her breast. His rigid flesh swelled beneath her hand. Samantha moaned again and curled

her elegant fingers around him, feeling the heat that—

"Sorry to interrupt you, mate. But we've been around the park twice now."

The enraptured occupants of the back seat jumped and looked up. Samantha yanked her hand out of Nick's lap, reaching up to pull his hand from her breast.

"Shall we give it another go?" the unrepentant cabbie asked, grinning at them in the rearview mirror.

Nick straightened and wrapped one arm around Samantha's shoulders, nestling her against his side. "Back to the hotel now, I think," he said calmly. He seemed totally unembarrassed at having been observed.

Samantha, however, turned her head into Nick's shoulder, hiding her flushed cheeks behind her cloud of silvery, spun-sugar hair.

"He's seen a lot more than we've just shown him," Nick whispered into the top of her head.

"But he hasn't seen me doing it," Samantha protested, her voice muffled against his shoulder.

Nick kissed her hair reassuringly. And then, as she raised her head, his lips grazed her temple. And the corner of her eye. A second later, he shifted on the seat and his lips wandered down her cheek.

"Hate to interrupt you again, mate. But we're here."

Nick sighed and drew away from her, frustrated laughter shaking his shoulders. Their eyes met. Not-so-cool gray and hot-coffee brown. His laughter stilled. "I'm asking again," he said lowly. "Now."

"And I'm saying yes," she answered, equally lowly. There wasn't anything else she could say. Not now. Not feeling the way she did about him.

He nodded once and drew away from her, pulling her satin coat up around her shoulders as he moved. His hands lifted to her nape, freeing her hair from the collar, and then he slid across the seat to open the door of the taxi. After paying the fare, he turned, like the gentleman he was, and assisted her to alight.

They walked, side by side, across the quiet lobby to the bank of elevators at the back wall. The small box was crowded with other returning hotel guests and they stood silently, touching lightly, electrically, at shoulder and hip and thigh, not talking because there were other people present and because, somehow, they didn't need to. The doors slid open on her floor. Still silent, still touching lightly, they walked down the hall to her room. She opened her evening purse and handed him her key.

He hesitated before taking it, feeling suddenly as if, in accepting it, he was also accepting something more. Something he'd never been willing to accept from a woman before. "Are you sure, Samantha?"

She looked up, startled by his question. How could he ask that now? How could he not know how she felt? How could he not see how sure she was?

Oh, she was a little bit frightened, in an excited kind of way. A little bit uncertain as to just where all this wonderful emotion would ultimately lead. But she was sure that she wanted to find out.

And then, in a blinding flash of intuition, she realized that Nick had asked the question because *he* wasn't sure. Not physically, of course. Physically, he knew exactly what he wanted. It was his emotions that he wasn't sure of, as if some part of him feared whatever their lovemaking would bring.

But she was sure enough for both of them.

She reached for his hand, lifting it in both of hers, and repeated the gesture that he'd made earlier that day. "I'm sure, Nick," she said, pressing the key into his palm.

He took the key and opened the door, gallantly ushering her ahead of him, appalled at the way his heart was racing. *Take it slow*, he told himself. *Go easy. It's just sex.* But before the door had clicked closed behind them, he was reaching for her.

His hard arms slid around her possessively, his hands hot on the exposed skin of her back. Samantha lifted her own arms eagerly, wrapping them around his neck to bring his mouth down to hers, unaware of the satin coat that fell from her shoulders to lay in a black and emerald heap at her feet, or the clutch purse that slipped from her fingers. All she was aware of at that moment, all she cared about, was the magnificent man in her arms and the wonderful way he made her feel. She gave herself up to him willingly, silently demanding that he give himself up to her as well.

His tongue invaded her mouth with leashed aggression, teasing at hers with gentle thrusts. Maddeningly, though, each time her tongue snaked out to meet his, his retreated, withdrawing to lick at the corners of her mouth, at her finely chiseled jawline, at the delicate lobe of her ear, tasting her with delicious torment. His lips refused to settle anywhere long enough to satisfy, only long enough to drive the flame of their mutual desire even higher.

Her hands feathered through his hair, touching his ears and nape, caressing his strong shoulders. His hands stroked slowly up and down the bare length of her spine, his touch as light as the teasing, nibbling kisses that he rained on her face and throat and the tops of her shoulders.

"Have I told you how much I like this dress?" he murmured into the smooth skin of her throat.

She nodded, inarticulate with the emotions created by his lips and hands and the irresistible caress of his warm, melodic voice.

"It amazes me how a dress can be so sexy and so ladylike at the same time." His fingertips met at the small of her back, moved tantalizingly up along the edges of the dress on each side of her body to just touch the outer curve of her breasts, and then back down again as he spoke. "It could drive a man to acts of ecstasy. *You* could drive a man to ecstasy, just by being."

Samantha shivered in sensual delight. His words, as much as the touch of his hands and lips, were arousing her to a fever pitch. "Nick." Her fingers curled on his shoulders, tugging impatiently at the fabric of his suit jacket.

"Hmm?" His Sambuca-scented breath warm against her neck. His hands were warm on her back.

Samantha grasped his hair, pulling his head up. "Kiss me," she demanded fiercely. "Now."

It was Nick's turn to shiver in helpless response. "Oh, so *that's* what you want," he murmured, deliberately resisting the pull of her hands in his hair—and the blazing need that made him want to crush her mouth under his. His eyes glinted down at her, alight with tenderness and hunger and a kind of gratified male laughter at her passionate ferocity. "You should have said so before."

She yanked on his hair. "Nick!" There was need in her demand. And impatience. And a desire more than hot enough to match his own.

He groaned and gave in, his head descending, his mouth opening over hers as if he would devour her whole. His hands moved lower on her back, curving down to cup the firm roundness of her bottom. He took a step back, bracing his body against the wall, and pulled her into the *V* of his splayed legs.

She could feel the hard length of his aroused body pressed intimately against her abdomen, and she surged forward, her supple body pressing against his, her arms tight around his neck, her mouth avid under his.

He moaned and shifted in her embrace, loosening his hold, and slid both hands between them to close hungrily over her small breasts.

A feeling of intense pleasure shot through her at his touch and she gasped into his mouth as his gentle, skillful fingers found the flowering buds of her nipples and finessed them to aching hardness. Before she could catch her breath his hands moved again, going to the tiny straps that held up her dress. Still kissing her, he began to ease them down off her shoulders.

The phone rang, causing them both to jump.

"Damn," he said.

"Maybe it will stop," she said hopefully. "Somebody's probably rung the wrong room." It rang twice more before she shifted away from him to answer it. "It might be an emergency," she apologized, switching on the bedside lamp. Late-night calls were usually emergencies. Nobody called this late with good news.

"Hello?" She frowned. "Robbie? What are you doing calling at this time of night? What's the matter?" Her frown deepened at his answer. "No, I'm fine. Yes." She glanced at Nick. "Yes. We—I just got in." Another glance at Nick. "Yes, I'm going straight to bed," she said, blushing a bit when Nick gave her a knowing look. "What?" She forced her eyes away from Nick's. "No. I promise, I won't look like a hag tomorrow. No, Robbie. Not now. Good night." She hung up the phone with a bit more force than necessary. "That was Robbie."

"So I gathered." Nick's voice was dry. He bent over and picked up her evening coat and purse, placing them on a chair. "Checking up on you?"

"Yes," she admitted ruefully. "He worries about me," she explained. "He always has, ever since we were teenagers."

"You don't have to explain anything to me, Samantha."

"I don't have a past with Robbie. Not that ki—"

He cut her off, unwilling to hear the rest of whatever she was going to say. "You don't need to explain Robbie to me," he said again, trying to believe it. The look he gave her was part relief, part regret. "Shall I go?"

"Go?" Samantha looked up at him, startled. Why would he want to go? Now, of all times?

"When we make love for the first time I don't want to have you worrying about some old boyfriend interrupting at the most inopportune moment."

Robbie isn't my old boyfriend, Samantha wanted to say. But then she reconsidered. For some reason, Nick seemed to want to believe that he was. She didn't know why, and she didn't like it much but what harm could it do—for a while, anyway? She crossed the small space between them and clasped her hands behind his neck. "We could take the phone off the hook," she suggested, peering up at him from under her lashes. A provocative half smile curved her perfect lips. "And hang out the Do Not Disturb sign."

Almost against his will, Nick responded. His arms tightened around her, gathering her close against his hard length for a long moment. She felt him take a deep ragged breath, his powerful chest lifting against her breasts, and then his arms loosened, and he reached up, tilting her chin with the tip of one finger. "I'll hang out the Do Not Disturb sign," he said. "While I'm doing that would you like to go into the bathroom and—" he paused for a split second, smiling briefly at the cliché he was about to utter, "—slip into something more comfortable?"

"Yes." Samantha nodded solemnly, completely missing his little joke. "I'd like to change first."

"Go on, then." He kissed her quickly and let her go. "I'll be here, waiting for you."

Once in the bathroom, Samantha slipped out of her dress and shoes and pantyhose and slipped into her short, silky cherry-colored robe. Automatically, as if in a daze, she washed off her makeup and brushed her teeth and then stood in the middle of the bathroom, wondering what it was she was supposed to do next. *Slip into something comfortable,* he'd said. She looked at herself in the mirror with wide gray eyes. Was this robe the kind of thing he'd had in mind? It wasn't a very glamorous garment. Not very glamorous at all. And neither was her bare face, she thought, realizing that she'd washed all her makeup off without thinking.

Hurriedly, her hands shaking a little, she reached for the makeup that was spread untidily on the shelf above the sink. She applied the cosmetics lightly—a little mascara, a touch of blusher—just enough to enhance what nature had given her. Better, but not really glamorous or sexy. And definitely not the Sophisticated Lady.

Oh, well, she thought, *this is the real me—the way I really am.* And, hopefully, it was the real Samantha that Nick wanted.

But suddenly she was assailed by doubts. *Was* this the way Nick wanted her? Or did he really want the Sophisticated Lady? She was his creation, after all. His concept. Maybe his ideal.

What am I doing in this bathroom, undressed, with that man waiting for me in the bedroom?

He was her boss, after all. She hardly knew him, really. She should have told him she wasn't sure. She should have let him leave after Robbie called. She should have listened to her mother's warnings. Should have . . .

But it was too late now. She *was* in the bathroom, undressed, and he *was* waiting for her. And he wanted her, she reminded herself. Just like she wanted him. And she did want him. Desperately.

Squaring her shoulders, she tightened the sash of her robe around her slender waist, switched off the overhead light and pulled open the bathroom door. The bedroom was bathed in shades of gray, lit only by the glimmer of fog-shrouded street lights and the pale half moon shining in through the thin sheers at the windows.

She blinked owlishly. "Nick?"

"Over here."

Yes, she could see him now. He was in bed, sitting propped up against the pillows with his hands folded behind his head. His furred chest was dark and indistinct, the sheet at his waist pale and shimmering in contrast. He opened his arms and held them out to her.

"Come here," he said softly, his voice low and trembling in the darkness.

Samantha went to him. He lifted the sheet as her knees hit the bed, covering her with it as she sank down beside him, and gathered her into his arms. His big, warm body seemed to envelop her with tenderness as he folded himself around her. "You took so long I thought you'd changed your mind," he whispered raggedly against the top of her head.

Samantha snuggled down against his hair-covered chest with a deep, heartfelt sigh, all her doubts disappearing with the admission of his, dissolved by the warmth of his body and the comfort of his arms around her. "Never happen," she said, nuzzling her face into his chest, reveling in the feel of the soft, crinkly hairs against her cheek. She slipped an arm around his waist to hold him to her. "You'll never get away from me now."

He shifted, lifting her so that she lay on top of him. "I don't want to get away." His hands closed over her arms, urging her upward along his hard body. "Not now. Not yet." *Not ever.* "Kiss me," he demanded hoarsely, using action to hide his inner panic at that last thought.

Samantha complied eagerly. Slanting her face against his, she used her tongue and teeth and lips to drive him slowly crazy. Her cool, elegant hands traveled slowly across his smooth bare shoulders and up the strong column of his neck to cradle tenderly the leanness of his jaw. Her fingertips just touched his ears, making tiny, teasing circles along the whorled ridges.

She felt his hands slide down her back, smoothing the silky material of her robe to its hem, slipping underneath it to curve over her bare buttocks. She arched against him as he pressed her hips down and he groaned, the sound coming up from his throat into his mouth, so that she thought she could taste the husky sweetness of it. Slowly he rolled over, trapping her beneath him, their two heated bodies locked in a passionate ballet. Her arms went around his neck, clasping him to her with all her strength.

She could hardly breathe with him on top of her, nearly crushing her, and his mouth ravaging hers as if he meant to devour her. But she didn't care. She reveled in the solid weight of him as he pressed her into the mattress. She relished each slow thrust of his tongue into her mouth. She gloried in the feel of his hard, hairdusted legs as they tangled with hers.

"Let's get this off you," he whispered, rolling over again as he spoke. His hands were hot and feverish, but steady, as he urged her to sit astride him. Deliberately he reached over and switched on the bedside lamp before he reached for the lapels of her bright cherry-red robe.

He opened it slowly. The valley between her breasts was revealed first, along with her breastbone and a narrow wedge of her concave belly and the nest of hair at the juncture of her thighs. His eyes glowing like hot coals, he ran a finger from the hollow at the base of her throat to the pale blond curls that pressed against his belly.

Samantha sucked in her breath and arched into that light caress, her skin quivering in the wake of his descending finger.

"Yes," he murmured. "Yes." He opened the robe a bit more, revealing her small, pink nipples, puckered now with need, her delicate rib cage, the handspan of her waist, the prominent bones of her hips. And then a bit more, so that it slipped off her shoulders and down her arms, pooling behind her, silky and cool where it lay across his thighs.

"You're beautiful," he said on a shaky, indrawn breath. "So beautiful."

Samantha felt herself flush under his heated gaze and she had to resist the urge to cover herself. "I'm too skinny," she mumbled, feeling more exposed than she ever had in her life. Her hands came up despite her will, each of them covering a breast. "Too small."

Nick reached up and grasped her wrists, gently pulling her hands away, and placed her palms on her widespread thighs. "You're perfectly beautiful." He lifted his hands, skimming them, almost reverently, over her slender ivory body from neck to knees—grazing lightly over the slight swell of her breasts, the inward slope of her waist, the gentle curve of her hips, the smooth length of her firm, rounded thighs, and back up again. "Perfectly perfect," he murmured, and cupped her breasts.

They were small and delicate in his palms, infinitely precious, excitingly pale against the darkness of his skin. His thumbs touched her puckered nipples lightly, making her gasp and arch. His fingers curved around her back. "I want to taste you," he said, urging her forward until she was balanced over him on her hands and knees, bringing the bounty of her breasts to his lips. "Let me taste you."

He teased at the swollen peaks, his tongue slowly circling first one, then the other, all the while making low murmurs of satisfaction and pleasure, until she thought she couldn't stand another minute of such delicious, maddening torture. Arching helplessly against his marauding tongue, she silently, eloquently, pleaded for more. A small whimper escaped her as Nick opened his lips and took the aching, turgid nipple into the moist warmth of his mouth.

She whimpered again when he reached between their bodies, down to the shadowed apex of her thighs, and touched her. The sound turned to a moan as his fingers slid deeper and then deeper still, sending hot waves of feeling coursing through every part of her.

She had never felt like this before, hadn't known that such intense, heart-wrenching, soul-stealing pleasure existed. The heat of his mouth, pulling strongly at her breast, seemed to be connected directly to the hot slide of his fingers between her thighs. One feeling enhanced and heightened the other, sending flames of pleasure roaring along her nerve endings to heat her skin and her blood and even her very bones. Nothing had ever felt so good. Or so right. And it seemed to go on...and on...and on, until she knew she couldn't stand another second without collapsing on top of him like a rag doll. She uttered another low moan without being aware of it. And then another and another, until she was producing a steady, panting sound.

Nick was panting, too, his body straining for control as he listened to her low, keening sounds of pleasure. She was deliciously soft and pebbled against his tongue, incredibly slick and hot where his fingers touched her. Her hips were rotating mindlessly against his hand, driving him to the very brink of his control.

"Nick," she murmured brokenly. "Nick, please!"

"Just a minute." His voice was as broken as hers. "Give me just a minute." He shifted under her slightly, reaching out with his free hand toward the foil packet he'd placed on the nightstand.

"No." Samantha pressed against him. "You don't need that," she murmured, letting him know she was already protected.

"Then take what you want, Samantha," he urged raggedly. "Take me inside you."

Panting, eager, she squirmed lower, reaching between their heated bodies to push his hand away as she positioned him. And then she sank down with a gasp, driving him into her to the hilt. Her climax was almost instantaneous and she bit down on her bottom lip to stifle the scream that rose in her throat.

"No, don't hold it back. Let me hear it." He reached up, touching her mouth with his index finger. "Let me hear how I make you feel."

All control left him then and he rolled them both over without withdrawing from her still-convulsing body. Wrapping his arms around her, taking her lips in a searing, open-mouthed kiss, he drove his hips against hers. Deeper, harder, faster, until she cried out again, barely recovered from her first overwhelming orgasm before she was thrust into her second.

"Yes, love, yes," she heard him whisper against her neck. And then he groaned like a man wounded and stiffened in her arms, his powerful torso surging upward and away from her, his hips pressing strongly forward and down. "Oh, God, yes!"

He lowered himself after a moment, his weight supported on his elbows as he cradled her against his chest and pressed soft, grateful kisses into the curve of her shoulder and the side of her neck. She could feel the heavy, accelerated beat of his heart against the racing cadence of her own, the rasping intake of his breath in unison with hers as they struggled to steady their breathing.

Samantha burrowed her face into the mat of damp, curling hair on his chest and let the aftermath wash over her. "It's never been like that before," she whispered incredulously. "I've read about it being like that, but I never thought . . ." Her voice trailed off as he lifted his head from her neck to look down at her. His eyes—those beautiful hot-coffee eyes—burned into hers.

"Not for me, either," he said hesitantly, brushing damp strands of pale silvery hair back from her face, and repeated, "Not for me, either." He kissed her softly, all over her face—comforting, tender kisses meant to soothe and gentle—and then rolled sideways, adjusting their damp bodies so that she lay in the circle of his arm with her head pillowed on his shoulder.

"Go to sleep now, Samantha." He stroked her hair. "It's late. Go to sleep."

Samantha closed her eyes obediently. Content and replete, she snuggled against his side like a kitten in familiar hands. There were things she wanted to say to him, things she wanted him to say to her. New feelings to examine and explore and talk about. But it could wait until later. There was no rush. She drifted off to sleep with a deep, contented sigh, leaving Nick wide awake, wondering if he'd just gotten himself into the kind of emotional morass he had always made a point to avoid.

5

"TURN YOUR HEAD a little to the right, Sammie. That's it. Chin down. Perfect! Now give me that sexy pout. Yeah, that's it. Lick your lips. Again. You're hot now! Really cookin'. Perfect. Ab-so-lute-ly perfect!"

Robbie worked in a kind of trance, keeping up a steady stream of chatter as the camera shutter whirred. He held his hand out, fingers snapping, for another loaded camera when the one he held was empty, unaware of anything but the picture that filled his viewfinder. He didn't seem to realize that they'd been at it for nearly four hours now without a break. He didn't seem to get hungry or thirsty or tired, and it obviously didn't occur to him that anyone else might possibly be human, either.

Though Samantha appreciated the fact that he'd become easier to get along with these past few days now that he was involved with his camera, she was more than human enough to be starving. She was also having hallucinations involving tall glasses of ice-cold beer. And she had a crick in her neck from tilting her head at unnatural angles for so long.

"Robbie," she said, forgetting to look sexy.

"Don't talk," Robbie admonished without looking up. "It ruins the line of those luscious lips. Lick them again. That's it," he said as Samantha automatically obeyed him. "Now look over there at Taylor."

Taylor Jones, classically tall, dark and handsome in a burgundy silk dressing gown, stood with one broad shoulder propped against the gilt-edged mantel, gazing at Samantha. That was his job, basically, to stare at Samantha with varying degrees of affection and lust in his eyes.

He'd been doing an admirable job of it for days; he'd stared down at her as they strolled along Lambert Walk so that Robbie could shoot them with Big Ben in the background; he'd looked on indulgently, her mink coat over his arm, while a London schoolboy taught her to hold a cricket bat for Robbie's camera; he'd gazed into her eyes across a tiny table for two, pretending that a whole pubfull of people weren't watching as Robbie circled them with a whirring Nikon in his hands.

And now in the hotel room in Paris where they were shooting, he'd been holding his present, seemingly nonchalant pose for most of the morning. He had to be as tired as she was, thought Samantha. As they all were, except for the madman with the camera.

"Robbie," she said again, still holding her pose by the bed.

"Give him that come-hither look of yours, Sammie," Robbie instructed. "Make it really hot."

"Robbie, we're all—"

"Come on, simmer a little," he coaxed impatiently. "You're the Sophisticated Lady, in Paris with her lover. Let's see some heat."

Samantha sighed, silently vowing to take a break after this roll of film was shot, and tried to look as if she were simmering.

"Yes, that's it! You got it. Now, open the first few buttons. Drop your shoulder a bit. The other one. Let the top slide down. Slowly. Slowly," he crooned in loverlike tones. "That's it, Sammie. You're doin' it to me good now."

Nick stood, unnoticed, just inside the door of the plush hotel room and watched Samantha work. She was dressed in a pair of black silk men's pajamas that probably cost more than many people made in a month. Her silvery blond hair was brushed smooth, á la Lauren Bacall, caught up behind one ear with a diamond clip while the other was left free to fall over her eye. Her face was subtly, expertly made up with a full complement of *Sophisticated Lady* cosmetics. And he thought she looked no more beautiful than she had in her cherry-colored robe, with her glorious hair frizzed out around her shoulders and no makeup on at all. Less, he mused, because the invitation in her eyes as she looked at Taylor wasn't real. Enough to make a man start salivating with anticipation, perhaps, but still only a pale imitation of the real thing.

He knew because he had seen the real thing.

And *that* was enough to singe a man all the way to his soul. Enough to make him ache and burn so that he was forced to seek the soothing coolness of her touch again and again. Enough to make him ignore the dictates of his logical mind and follow the dictates of his hungering body.

And it *was* only his body that hungered, he assured himself for at least the hundredth time. He was, after all, a very physical man with a highly active sex drive. He enjoyed women, all kinds of women, once he had them pigeon-holed in the proper category.

There were women he dated and had physical relationships with—successful, ambitious career women, who wanted nothing more from him than an occasional escort and the mutual satisfaction of their mutual desire, or sophisticated socialites who knew how to play at love without letting their emotions get involved. There were women with whom his relationships were strictly platonic—business colleagues and family and the friends of his sisters. And then there were those women he didn't get involved with at all, the ones who were looking for husbands, or commitment, or love. He'd thought that Samantha belonged firmly in that first category.

She was successful, sophisticated and unbelievably sexy. A career woman. A New Yorker. But there was something else there, too. Something that went beyond the purely physical, inexplicably making him want more than the five glorious nights of passion they'd already shared.

He stared at her now, his gaze hard and searching, his expression rife with wariness and a curious kind of longing, wondering what it was about this slender, elegant woman that tempted him to want that dangerous something more from her. Something that he'd never wanted from any other woman.

Samantha looked up, as if feeling his stare, and her smile widened in a welcome that was his alone. Her gray eyes filled with warmth, making the invitation in her gaze very real. Nick caught his breath, dazzled by the honest emotion that shone in her face.

That was what made him want more from her.

He should break it off now, he told himself, before she became any more involved than she obviously already was. Before *he* became any more involved. Before things became emotional and messy.

But it was too late. Samantha was moving toward him, fairly flying across the plush white carpet, her elegant hands outstretched, her eyes shining with delight at seeing him so unexpectedly. He found himself holding out his hands to her, as if he had no will to do otherwise.

"Nick." His name on her lips was a caress. Her hands touched his. "I didn't expect you here until tomorrow."

He hadn't expected to be in Paris until tomorrow, either, but he couldn't make himself stay away from her any longer. "I was able to break away a little earlier than I expected."

"I'm glad." She gazed up at him with her whole heart in her eyes. "I missed you."

It had only been two days but he could see that it was true. She had missed him. The silent warnings flashed through his mind like lights at a railroad crossing but he ignored them. "How've you been?" he asked, unable to admit, even to himself, that he had missed her, too. "Busy?"

"Not busy enough," Samantha said, forgetting that Robbie had been working them all like dogs. "I've thought about you every minute I wasn't working." Her smile widened, emphasizing her sculpted cheekbones. "And even some when I was."

Nick laughed softly and squeezed her fingers. "I thought about you, too," he admitted before he could tell himself not to.

"Good thoughts?"

Nick's smile turned decadent. "Very good thoughts," he assured her.

"Mine were, too. I—"

"You're keeping everybody waiting, Sammie," Robbie complained loudly, interrupting her.

"No, she isn't," Taylor said before either Samantha or Nick could answer. He moved from his place by the mantel as he spoke and flopped his long body across the bed. "I'm ready for a break." He closed his eyes with mock weariness. "Everybody's ready for a break."

"We have three more outfits to do yet," Robbie reminded them.

"Just two." The production manager, Terri Gunnerson, seemed to summon the information from some mental notebook. "The white cashmere robe and that emerald-green caftan thing."

"Two. Three. What difference does it make?" Robbie said irritably, scowling at the camera in his hands. "We still have to get them done today."

"Agreed," said Terri. "But a ten-minute break isn't going to throw us off schedule."

"If we take ten minutes now, we'll run over into lunch," Robbie argued, his voice challenging as he faced the production manager.

"We're going to run into lunch anyway," Terri said. "Sammie's got to have her hair crimped for that caftan thing."

"Crimped!" Robbie sounded even more annoyed. "That takes too long."

"Too long for what?" Terri put her small, capable hands on her hips, fixing him with a piercing stare. "You're not going anywhere, are you?"

Robbie shrugged. "I just don't see why her hair has to be crimped."

"You don't have to see. You just have to take the pictures, okay? Besides—"

"Besides," Nick interrupted smoothly. "*I* want Samantha's hair crimped." He glanced down at the woman whose hands he still held. "It makes her look like an angel."

"And you're the boss, right?" Robbie's voice was perilously near a snarl.

Nick's glance snapped back to the younger man. Everyone else's followed expectantly. Ever since that first night in London, Robbie had been doing his level best to provoke Nick every chance he got. It was time he got slapped down for it. A part of Samantha hoped it would happen now, before things went any further. Another part cringed from any sort of confrontation between the two men. She had no doubt who would come out the winner, and Robbie's ego wasn't so strong that he could survive a public tongue lashing. He never had been.

"Right," Nick said easily, surprising them with his mildness. "I'm the boss." *And you would do well to remember that*, his look said.

Robbie glared at him sullenly, unwilling to back down but obviously afraid to push it.

"Well, uh—" Terri's voice broke the tense silence "—why don't we go ahead and shoot the white robe. Samantha's hair can stay the same for that, except for the diamond clip. Then we'll break for lunch before the caftan. Taylor—" she nudged the male model's leg with her foot, "—you need to change into that navy-blue robe."

He opened one eye. "Do I have to?"

"Yes, you have to." She nudged him again. "Move."

"Aw, Terri."

"Aw, yourself." She grabbed the navy-blue robe from the rack of designer clothes that stood in one corner of the room and tossed it at him. "Now move. You, too, Sammie," she said when Taylor had gotten to his feet. "I put your last two outfits in the bathroom."

"But I'm starving." Samantha stuck her bottom lip out, doing her part to smooth over the awkwardness that Robbie had caused.

"Be a good girl," Nick said, "and do what Terri tells you to. I have a surprise for you for lunch." His glance flickered around the room. "For all of you."

"What is it?" She looked up at him teasingly. "Frog legs? Liver pâté? Truffles?"

"Samantha, luv, please," Lulu reprimanded her. "Not frog legs." The makeup artist mimed sticking her finger down her throat. "Just the thought turns my stomach. Now, what I'd really like is a plate of bangers and mash. Plain, solid English food." She smacked her lips. "I don't like all this French food that I can't even pronounce."

"You can barely pronounce your own name," Jeffrey said in the uppercrust accent that was so at odds with his American cowboy appearance. Lulu pretended to look for something to throw at the hair stylist.

Samantha laughed, her glance darting to Robbie's sullen face. *See how much fun you could be having?* her look said as she stared at her stepbrother. But Robbie turned his head away, refusing to acknowledge her.

"All right, you guys." Terri grabbed the curling iron that Lulu was brandishing at Jeffrey. "Back to work, Samantha." Terri pointed at the bathroom door with her free hand. "Go get changed. The sooner we finish with the white robe, the sooner you can eat."

"Yes, ma'am." With a last, quick squeeze, Samantha slipped her fingers from Nick's and ducked into the luxurious bathroom. It was all sparkling white with gilt fixtures and a mirrored wall behind the huge sunken tub, as befit a bridal suite. She slipped out of the black pajamas, wondering idly what it was costing Gavino Cosmetics to rent the suite for the day, and reached for the white robe hanging on the back of the door on a padded hanger. Designed like a man's, it was fashioned from whisper-thin, sensuously soft cashmere. The notched lapel and turned-back cuffs were edged in smooth white satin. She slipped it over her bare skin, snugly overlapped the front edges and drew the sash tight around her slender waist.

"Oh, don't you look beautiful in that, luv," Lulu said when she came out of the bathroom. She waved her toward a chair by the open French doors that lead out onto the terrace. "Sit right here in the light."

Samantha sat as instructed, and had her face creamed and then re-done in a whole new color spectrum of Gavino Cosmetics. Lulu applied a delicate ivory base first and then pale gray eye shadow with the hint of navy liner and just a touch of shell pink blusher and lipstick. Jeffrey took over next, replacing the diamond clip with a pale pink ribbon that held her hair back from her face.

"This is sophisticated?" Samantha questioned, surveying her reflection with professional concern. She glanced up at the production manager. "Terry?"

"You look lovely," Terri said. "As usual. But you're right. Something's not quite right."

"Nick? What do you think?" Samantha lifted her eyes to the man who had moved across the room to stand beside her. Although the *Sophisticated Lady* campaign had been refined and brought to realization by a whole team of experts, the original concept had been his. He should know best how she should look.

Nick reached out, lifting her chin with his forefinger and studied her upturned face. She looked like a storybook bride—young, innocent and radiantly beautiful. And not at all sophisticated. It was unnerving.

"Does anyone have a pair of glasses?" he asked a little hoarsely.

"Glasses?" Samantha echoed vaguely, distracted by the huskiness of his voice. He sounded like that in bed, when he was whispering to her, when he was holding her so close that she couldn't tell where she stopped and he began. Desire pierced her sharply, making her weak with longing. Two days was too long.

"Something horn-rimmed and heavy," she heard him say. His voice sounded to her as if it were blanketed in a thick fog.

Lulu had a pair of glasses, heavy, black ones with plain window glass in the frames that she used strictly as a fashion accessory.

"We'll need a paper, too," Nick said, taking the glasses from the makeup artist to slip onto the bridge of Samantha's perfect nose. "The *Wall Street Journal*, if you can find one." He took Samantha's hand and led her out onto the balcony. Placing his hands on her shoulders, he sat her down at the small, linen-covered table that Terri had set for "breakfast."

There were two gold-rimmed white china place settings, a silver-plated pot of coffee, two halves of a picture-perfect grapefruit and a napkin-lined basket of croissants that had been sprayed with a glaze to keep them fresh-looking for as many hours as they were needed.

"Pretend you're reading," Nick said, putting the *Wall Street Journal* into her hands. "You're a business woman, here in Paris for a conference. Chemicals." He nodded to himself. "Yes, you're a chemical engineer and Taylor—" he indicated the robe-clad man who had taken the seat opposite her "—Taylor is your husband. No, your lover," he amended, surprised at the spurt of jealousy that surged through him at the thought of either being true. He stepped back, surveying her.

She looked up at him, owl-eyed behind the glasses, her expression anything but cool and remote. Anything but innocent.

But something still wasn't right. She still looked like a bride. He reached out, snagging one finger in the modest, narrow V made by the lapels of her robe, and tugged the neckline a bit wider and lower, partially exposing the inner curves of her small, perfect breasts.

Samantha sat stone still, paralyzed by his touch, feeling as if he'd left a blazing trail of fire down the middle of her chest. Her nipples hardened against the soft, thin cashmere that covered her. Her insides heated, melting together in an exquisite fusion of pure feeling. Two days was *far* too long.

"That's the look I want," Nick said softly, devouring her with his dark eyes.

She knew instinctively that he wasn't only talking about the here and now. He was seeing her as she had been and as he wanted her again. As she wanted to be. Naked in his arms with her silvery hair fanned out across the pillow and her breasts swollen and aching for his touch.

"Just exactly that look," he whispered. His finger was still hooked in the V of her robe, his eyes were riveted to hers.

Samantha reached up, trancelike, to touch the back of his hand. She pressed it lightly, longingly, against her.

Taylor crossed his legs and looked away.

Terri cleared her throat.

Lulu sighed.

Robbie snarled into his camera. "If we're going to finish this before dark, we'd better get to it," he said roughly, breaking the spell that held them.

Without a word, his eyes never leaving hers, Nick slipped his hand out from under her fingers and stepped out of the range of the viewfinder.

Robbie was stiff and silent during the first few shots but, gradually, he became lost in his camera and the woman framed in the viewfinder. "That's it, Sammie," he said, talking more to himself and his camera than to her. "Pick up the coffee cup now. Look over at Taylor. That's it. Smolder a little. Perfect."

If she was smoldering, it wasn't for Robbie or his camera or the theatrically handsome man sitting across the table from her. It was for the dark man standing just out of camera range, staring at her with an equally smoldering look in his own eyes.

"Push those glasses up on your nose. They're slipping. Okay, now, look like you're reading the paper. Give me intelligent, Sammie. Intelligent and sexy. Yes! That's it." Robbie circled around the table, shooting them from an angle that captured the Eiffel Tower in the background. "Lean toward Taylor a little, like you're showing him something in the paper. That's it. Perfect."

Samantha automatically responded to his voice, following his crooning instructions as if she were in a daze. Looking up, looking down, holding the coffee cup to her lips without smearing her lipstick, smiling seductively at Taylor, pretending an avid interest in the stock prices in the paper, but she was really only aware of Nick and the expression in his dark, hot-coffee eyes.

Later, when they were back in New York, when her face was plastered all over every major fashion magazine, these pictures would be judged to be the very best of the entire *Sophisticated Lady* campaign. "There's a certain look in her eyes," more than one person would say enviously.

"Sammie." Someone waved a hand in front of her face. "Yoo-hoo, Sammie, lunch is here."

Samantha blinked. Taylor was no longer in the seat across from her. Robbie stood in the open French doors, his expression sullen again as he fiddled with his camera. A uniformed bellhop was fussing around a linen-draped cart in the gilt and white room behind him, surrounded by the rest of the crew as he lifted silver covers with a flourish. Nothing seemed real. Nothing but Nick.

He moved across the small space that separated them and cupped his hand under her elbow to lift her from the wrought-iron chair. "Your surprise lunch is here," he murmured, fighting the urge to scoop her up in his arms and bundle her out of the bridal suite to his own room. She looked so deliciously receptive with that soft, dreamy look on her face. So warm. So giving. "Aren't you even interested in what it is?" he asked.

"Cheeseburgers!" Lulu squealed from inside the room. "Cheeseburgers and chocolate shakes."

"I'm not very hungry," Samantha said, for the first time in her life completely uninterested in the prospect of food.

Nick grinned. "Come on in and take a sniff." He steered her past Robbie, where he stood blocking the open doorway, and around the chairs the others had pulled up to the room service cart. "I guarantee you'll get your appetite back. And if you don't—" he guided her to a brocade love seat and sat down beside her

"—I'll order you something else." He leaned close. "Some frog legs, maybe. Authentic frog legs."

The smile they shared was loverlike and secret, reminding Samantha of past pleasures, whispering promises of the delights still to come.

"I've got an errand to run," Robbie announced loudly, breaking the spell that bound them.

Samantha looked around. "Aren't you going to eat?"

Robbie shook his head. "Got an errand to run," he repeated.

"Don't be gone long," Terri warned, casually wiping hamburger juice from her chin with the back of her hand. "We aren't going to spend much time eating."

"Don't worry about it. I'll be back in plenty of time." The door slammed behind him.

"What's the matter with *him*?" Terri asked. "He's been the most diffi—" she glanced at Samantha. Everyone knew by now that Robbie was her stepbrother.

"You don't have to be tactful on my account." Samantha poked at her thick chocolate shake with a straw, still unable to work up an appetite. "He's definitely been a little difficult these past couple of days."

Lulu snorted. "He's been in a royal snit from the beginning, he has."

"Something must be bothering him," Samantha offered, careful to avoid Nick's knowing eyes. She knew, all too well, that he thought she was what was bothering her stepbrother. "He's not usually so—" she hesitated, searching for a word that wouldn't sound too condemning "—temperamental."

"That's certainly putting it mildly," Taylor said unexpectedly. He was lying full length across the pale blue satin spread with his hands folded across his stomach and his eyes closed as if napping.

Nick gave him a considering look. "Why do you say that?" The question was casual but his eyes, above the cheeseburger he lifted to his mouth, were anything but.

"Robbie Lowell may be a genius when it comes to taking pictures of beautiful women," Taylor said, his eyes still closed. "But he's a pain in the ass to work with." An eye flickered open. "Sorry, Sammie," he apologized, "but he is."

"Not always," Samantha defended the absent Robbie loyally. "He's just nervous about this job, that's all. It makes him act like—"

"A pain in the ass," said Taylor.

"Taylor!"

"It's true. I've worked with him five, maybe six times since I started modeling." The male model levered himself up on to an elbow. "How many times have you worked with him?"

"Dozens of times," Samantha said. "He took most of the pictures in my book."

"On a job?"

"Well, no," she admitted, realizing that it was true. She leaned forward and put her unfinished milkshake on the linen-draped room service cart just as Jeffrey finished his cheeseburger. He got up and came around behind her to begin crimping her hair. "This is the first time we've actually worked together."

"Well, you can take my word for it. He's totally neurotic when he's working."

"He can't be all that bad," Jeffrey said through the rat-tailed comb in his teeth. He removed it, carefully lifting a section of hair with the end. "He obviously keeps getting hired."

"Because he's good. Damned good," Taylor admitted grudgingly. "But one of these days being good isn't going to be enough and someone's going to can him. It's happened once already."

Samantha bristled. "Robbie's never been fired!"

"What about the Bellamy account?" Taylor asked.

Nick frowned. "Bellamy account?" he prompted.

"He wasn't fired from the Bellamy account," Samantha said indignantly. "It was a case of irreconcilable differences with the art director."

Jeffrey tugged gently on her hair. "Sit still," he admonished. "You're going to make me burn one of us with this thing."

"Sorry." Samantha stilled and straightened but there was fire in her eyes. "His leaving was a mutual decision," she stated firmly. "Robbie told me all about it."

"Wasn't there some sort of dust-up on the Bellamy account?" Terri said. "I don't remember exactly. Something about..." she shook her head, unable to call whatever it was to mind.

"Well, Peggy Keegan, who rooms with Cassie Moore, who was one of the models on that account, told me that it had more to do with Robbie's attitude and unreliability than any 'artistic dispute,'" Taylor said, all too happy to fill everyone in.

"Gossip!" Samantha said disdainfully. "Everyone in this business thrives on it. But you can take it from me, Robbie is *not* unreliable."

Deliberately Taylor looked around the opulent suite. "He isn't here, is he?" He dropped his head back onto the satin spread and closed his eyes as if the conversation were over.

"He'll be here in plenty of time," Samantha said.

"He'd better be," Terri added. She scowled down at the Mickey Mouse watch on her wrist. "If we finish this session before one, we'll have the rest of the afternoon free before we have to start the night shoot. And I, for one, intend to catch up on my sleep."

"Sightseeing for me," Samantha said, glad that the conversation had gotten away from the subject of Robbie.

"Whatever." Terri crossed the room for her clipboard, nudging Taylor as she passed the bed. "You need to get into that black velvet smoking jacket. With the white silk shirt and the ascot. No, not the ascot," she corrected herself. "We decided that looked too prissy, didn't we?" She reached behind her ear for something to make notes with and encountered only hair. "Anybody seen my Cross pen?" she asked, patting her shirt pocket. "Damn, I told Dad I'd only lose it." She pushed around the papers on a small gilt-edged desk.

Lulu stuck an eyebrow pencil under her nose.

"Thanks," she said absently, her eyes on the clipboard. "Okay, Taylor, you're in the smoking jacket. Samantha you're in that green caftan thing. It's in the bathroom. Jeffrey can finish your hair after you've changed." She made a checkmark. "Lulu, you're going to need the *Midnight Eyeshadow Collection* and the *Nightblooming Rose* lipstick and blusher for this one. Go for glamorous and sultry. Nick, why don't you push that cart out of the way?" she continued, as if he were one of her minions.

The door to the hallway opened.

"Good, you're back," Terri said as Robbie entered the room. "You need to get set up over there in front of the fireplace." She waved one hand. "Help Nick get that stuff cleared away."

"Get your errand taken care of?" Nick asked as Robbie reluctantly did as he was bid.

To the casual observer there was nothing the least bit ominous in the question. But Samantha wasn't a casual observer and she could see the keen, almost calculating interest that lurked behind it.

"Yeah, I got it done." Robbie's voice was noncommittal and bland.

Too bland, Samantha thought. His eyes had a feverish, glow—half triumphant, half furtive. His face was flushed. He seemed, somehow, to be on fire, as if he could hardly contain some secret excitement. Samantha hadn't seen that look in a long, long time but she was very much afraid that she knew what it meant. It gave her a sick, sinking feeling in her stomach.

"Listen, Terri," he said enthusiastically. "I've got a great idea for this shot. What if we . . ."

SAMANTHA CHANGED immediately after the last click of Robbie's camera, rushing into the bathroom to trade the flowing emerald silk caftan for slim black leather pants and an oversized scarlet sweater decorated with abstract slashes of royal purple. She automatically fluffed out her crimped hair and toned down her makeup, a worried frown between her arched brows as she wondered how she was going to get Robbie alone for a few minutes. She had to talk to him. Now. Before what she desperately hoped hadn't already happened went any further.

Only Nick and Robbie were left in the bridal suite when she came out of the bathroom. Robbie was fiddling with his camera, fitting on a wide-angle lense. Nick was leaning against the open doorjamb, his suit coat pushed back, his hands in his trouser pockets, a keen, considering look on his face as he watched the younger man.

"Well, here I am," Samantha said, a bright smile plastered on her face as she greeted the two men.

Nick straightened, smiling as he took in her sleek pants and brightly colored sweater. "I guess I'll need to go back to my room to change if you want to go sightseeing." He was wearing his usual elegant suit and tie. "Want to come up and keep me company?"

Samantha avoided his eyes. "In a minute," she said. "I need to talk to Robbie first. Uh, family stuff," she improvised, feeling as if the lie was emblazoned on her forehead. "I'll meet you in—" she glanced at her watch "—ten minutes?"

"I'll wait." His voice stayed the same but his eyes lost some of their warmth as they darted between Samantha and the photographer. He recognized guilt when he saw it. He knew a lie when he heard it, too. And he didn't like it, not from anyone, but especially not from her.

"No, that's all right," she said. "I'll only be a minute. You go ahead." She smiled and playfully waved him out. "Go on."

He wavered for a second, wanting to confront them about it—whatever *it* was. But what, really, was there to confront them about other than a gut feeling that she was hiding something from him? "Ten minutes," he warned and left them alone in the bridal suite.

Samantha rounded on her stepbrother the second the door was closed. "All right, Robbie, where is it? What did you steal this time?"

6

"STEAL?" Robbie said indignantly, staring at her as if she'd lost her mind. "What do you mean, steal? I haven't stolen anything!"

"Don't lie to me, Robbie."

"I'm not lying. I haven't stolen anything!"

But she knew he had. All the signs were there, exactly as they'd been years ago, falling into a disturbingly familiar pattern—the growing insecurity covered by a brooding surliness, the suppressed excitement of doing the forbidden, the furtiveness, the blustering denial, the equally blustering confession, and then, finally, the remorse and shame.

"Don't make such a big deal out of it, Sammie," he said negligently. "It's just a little recreational shoplifting."

"Recreational shoplifting? It's *stealing*!" Her voice rose on the last word and she lowered it, looking around the room as if someone might have overheard her. "Do you know what could happen to you if you were arrested in a foreign country?" she went on in a lower tone. "We're not in the United States, Robbie. They could toss you in jail and throw away the key."

"You've seen too many movies." He picked up his camera and circled her, snapping off pictures while she tried to reason with him.

"Robbie, this is serious. And it affects all of us. Not just you, but everyone on this shoot." She slapped at him. "Will you stop that and listen to me? We could all get in trouble for what you've done."

He shrugged, still snapping pictures.

"I can't let that happen, Robbie."

That got his attention. He lowered his camera. "You're not going to fink on me, are you, Sammie?"

"Give me one good reason why I shouldn't."

He smiled at her engagingly, a little boy trying to charm his mother when he'd been caught with his hand in the cookie jar. "Family loyalty?" he suggested.

Samantha shook her head.

Robbie dropped the fake charm. "Hell, it was just an isolated incident. A one-time thing. You know, for a kick."

"For a kick? You shoplifted for a *kick*?"

He shrugged. "Call it a relapse, if that'll make you feel better."

"Oh, Robbie, please! The only thing that will make me feel better is if you don't do it again."

"I won't do it again," he said promptly, smirking.

Samantha scowled at him, upset and unamused.

Robbie sighed. "I mean it, Sammie," he said with an air of resignation. "Really, I won't do it again." He drew a cross in the air over his heart. "I swear it."

"How do I know you won't do it again? Even if you mean it, how do *you* know you won't do it again? Remember what the psychologist said about—"

"Oh, don't give me that psychology crap! This is nothing like that. I was a little depressed, okay? And I cheered myself up. This job is enough to depress anyone."

Samantha stared at him, stupefied. "But the job is going great."

"Yeah, but for how long? Gavino only hired me because of you."

"That's not true!"

"Oh, come on, Sammie. Gavino wanted you. He knew you wanted me for this job." He glared at her, looking part hurt little boy, part defiant adolescent, part unhappy man. "So he played the big shot and gave his little tootsie what she wanted."

"Oh, Robbie, that's crazy and you know it." She ignored the taunt, knowing he was only trying to sidetrack her. "Nick didn't hire you because of me. If anything, it's the other way round. It was your pictures that got *me* this job, remember?"

But it was no use. She could see that Robbie wasn't paying any attention to the logic of her argument. His deep-seated insecurities had no logic when he got like this.

"Okay, look," she said. "Suppose Nick did only hire you because of me. It's totally wrong but let's just pretend that you're right. How long do you think you'll keep this job if Nick finds out that you've been shoplifting?"

"Are you going to tell him?" There was no smart-aleck adolescent in his voice now. "Are you, Sammie?"

She hesitated. She *should* tell Nick. As their employer, he had a right to know if there was a potential problem on the shoot. As her lover, well, she simply *wanted* to tell him. "I might—" she began.

Robbie flung his camera on the bed and grasped her hands in a punishing grip. "You wouldn't really, would you, Sammie?" He was no longer defiant. "It wasn't much. Just some chocolates and a couple of belts and a manicure kit. That's all, nothing big. I—"

"Chocolates?" she said, staring at him. "You don't even like chocolate. Why...?"

But she knew why. He hadn't needed any of the things he'd stolen before, either; people who shoplifted for emotional reasons rarely did so out of real need. It was emotional turmoil that triggered the crime; major insecurities, life-threatening illness or the loss of a loved one through death or divorce, usually.

"The poor fool's in love with you."

Samantha's eyes widened as Nick's words echoed in her head. Was Nick right, after all? Was her stepbrother in love with her? Was "losing" her to Nick why he had reverted to old, unhappy habits?

"I'll return everything," Robbie said. "I'll . . . I'll send it back anonymously. And I won't do it again. I promise." He sounded like a kid who was afraid somebody was going to tell his mother that he'd been smoking cigarettes and reading *Hustler* behind the garage. "Just don't tell."

Samantha sighed, relieved by Robbie's manner. Nick was wrong, she decided. What Robbie felt for her was exactly what every brother felt for his older sister. It just seemed like more to Nick because he didn't understand Robbie's complicated emotional problems.

"All right, Robbie. I won't tell," she said, patting his hands comfortingly. "But there are conditions."

"Anything!"

"First, you return what you took."

"I'll send it back today," he agreed hurriedly. "What else?"

"You have to promise to tell me when the urge comes over you again. No." She touched her fingers to his mouth to stop him speaking. "I know it's not something you can control all by yourself. You need help. Do you promise?"

Robbie nodded warily. "What's the third condition?"

"That you also promise to get professional help when we get back to New York."

"And you promise not to tell?"

"I . . ." she hesitated.

"Sammie, promise me!"

"I promise," she said solemnly, knowing she was going to regret it.

LATE AFTERNOON SUNLIGHT filtered through the gauzy curtains at the long windows, scattering hazy spears of light across the plush, pale gray carpet and the pile of blankets that lay in a crumpled heap at the foot of the bed. The pale wavering light continued all the way across the king-size bed, striping the two languid bodies entwined on the rumpled, wine-colored sheets with flickering lozenges of dark and light.

Samantha lay on her side, her head pillowed on Nick's arm, her hand playing lightly over the damp, curling hairs on his chest. Her body felt deliciously replete but her mind was alert and active, whirling with a myriad of emotions. Remnants of anger and sadness. Lingering passion. Love. Guilt.

When had she become so good at evasion?

"Family matter all taken care of?" Nick had asked when he'd opened the door to her knock.

"Umm-hmm."

"Robbie isn't in any trouble, is he?"

"Oh, no. Nothing like that." She'd smiled brightly—too brightly, she knew—and slipped her arm through his, peeking up at him from beneath her lashes. "Are we going sight-seeing now?"

Nick looked at her for a moment, his expression unreadable. She'd thought she'd seen suspicion in the brief moment before she looked away, but that was probably a product of her guilty conscience.

He'd reached up, cupping her cheek in his hand so that her face was turned to his. "I'd like to help if there's a problem."

"No problem. Really," she'd murmured wretchedly, unable to meet his eyes. She hated lying to him but she'd promised Robbie. "But thank you for asking." She'd turned her lips into his palm, in a gesture of gratitude, really, but something changed when her mouth touched him.

They both went very still.

"Samantha?"

She'd lifted her suddenly heavy lids slowly. "I'm not really all that interested in sight-seeing." Her tongue flickered out to lick the center of his palm. "Are you?"

He hadn't been, either, and in minutes they'd ended up on the big bed, gasping and plunging toward a glorious climax that left Samantha physically sated, emotionally unsatisfied, and feeling as guilty as if she'd deliberately used sex to divert Nick from what she didn't want him knowing about. And the most awful thing was, she wasn't all that certain that she hadn't done exactly that.

But, then, hadn't he done exactly the same thing to her? And more than once?

She'd tried to tell him, more than once, how she felt about him—how something inside her lit up and came to life when he was near—how it made her smile to herself just to think of him. And each time she'd tried, he'd stopped her with a kiss. Or a touch. Or a hot, whispered word. And if that wasn't using sex, she didn't know what was.

So she'd held back from making a declaration of her feelings, some heretofore-uncalled-upon caution warning her that he wasn't ready to hear what she wanted so desperately to tell him. She'd thought at first that, like so many men, he was just wary of a commitment. With his background, he certainly had a right to be wary. But there was more, she was sure. Something he wasn't telling her. The thought that he was hiding something, too, made her feel a little less guilty but no happier with the situation.

"You never did tell me what Robbie's problem was." Nick's voice came from somewhere above her head. His fingers languidly stroked the long curve of her back.

Samantha's hand stilled against his chest. *Tell him*, she thought. *Tell him.* "I never said he had a problem," she said instead.

Nick shifted, turning on his side to face her more fully. "You didn't have to say anything, Samantha. I have eyes."

She plucked at the hairs on his chest and said nothing.

Nick sighed. "Is it drugs?"

Samantha's eyes flickered to his. "No, of course not."

"He's got all the symptoms."

Samantha levered herself up onto an elbow to look down at her lover. "He does not," she said with a touch of indignation.

Nick stared up at her with hard, piercing eyes. "You wouldn't lie to me, would you?"

Samantha reared back a little. "Robbie is not on drugs," she stated with complete conviction, neatly avoiding the question of lying.

"He has all the symptoms," Nick repeated.

"Symptoms?"

"The mood swings. The furtiveness. The flushed face and feverish eyes when he came back from his little 'errand.' Sure he didn't run out for a quick snort?"

"He is *not* on drugs," she said vehemently, glad she was able to answer him so positively on this. She pushed herself fully upright, coming to her knees beside Nick's recumbent body. Her small breasts swayed enticingly with the movement. "And he never has been. It's just—" she waved one hand in the air "—artistic temperament, that's all."

"Really?" he said dryly.

"Yes, really." She raised her chin imperiously and tossed back the tangled hair that fell over her flushed cheeks. "And I resent your implication otherwise."

"I wasn't aware that I had made anything so mild as a mere implication," Nick said, amused. He'd never seen her angry before; it was an intriguing and arousing sight. "I thought I'd stated my suspicions quite clearly."

"Well, you can take your suspicions and . . . and . . ." Samantha sputtered to a stop, unable to sort through all the conflicting emotions that assailed her—righteous indignation that Nick would accuse Robbie of drug use—guilt at what she was really hiding from him—irrational anger at them both for putting her in this position—and, overlaying it all, a vague sense of hurt because of the words he hadn't said and the feelings he wouldn't allow her to express. "Oh, never mind!" She flung up her hands and turned away from him.

Nick grabbed her flailing arm. "Now don't get upset," he said, enjoying himself. "I wasn't accusing *you* of anything."

Samantha jerked out of his grasp and rolled to her feet beside the bed. She seemed unaware of her nakedness—and his. "You were accusing Robbie. Which is just the same as accusing me." It wasn't, of course, but she was too fired up to be rational. "Well, I'm not going to stand around, listening to any more of it," she said, looking for her scattered clothes. They blazed a haphazard trail from the doorway to the edge of the bed. She bent down to scoop up her red lace panties.

Nick reached out, grabbed her wrist, and yanked. She fell heavily, her body sprawling over his. He turned with her in his arms, twisting so that she was suddenly looking up at him.

She glared at him. "Let me up."

Nick grinned. "Not on your life."

Samantha pushed against his bare shoulders. "Let me up, right now!"

"Uh-uh." He captured both her hands, pinning them to the mattress on either side of her head. "You're a real little tiger when you get riled, aren't you?" he said admiringly, a wolfish grin still lighting up his dark face. He'd forgotten all about Robbie and his problems and the rest of the world entirely. His whole attention was focused on the beautifully flushed, angry woman under him, squirming for all she was worth.

Samantha kicked her feet, trying to knee him where it would do the most good.

Nick laughed softly, seductively, and threw one leg over hers to still them.

"Damn you, Nick. I don't think this is the least bit funny!" She tried to twist her wrists out of his grasp, bucking with her hips to dislodge him, but succeeded only in tiring herself. She subsided, glaring at him, her chest heaving, her breath coming in quick pants. "This isn't fair, you know," she said at last, trying for a tone of extreme reasonableness.

"I know," he agreed smugly.

"Then let me up."

He shook his head.

All reasonableness fled. "Let me up! Right now, Nick! I mean it! If you don't let me up right this minute, I'll never speak to you again."

"Yes, you will." He bent his head, his lips just brushing against her throat.

Samantha tried to conk him with her chin.

He moved lower and his tongue snaked out, tracing a line down the middle of her chest.

"Nick, dammit! Let me go!" She thrashed wildly against him, managed to get one hand free, and yanked his hair.

Nick grunted. "Ah, ah, none of that now." Casually he captured her wrist again and brought both of her hands up over her head. Pinning them there with one of his, he reached sideways with the other, groping for something on the floor.

"Nick, what are you doing? What—" She broke off abruptly as something cool and smooth slithered across her face. She saw a flash of red silk. *His tie*, she thought. And then he lifted her hands and began wrapping it around her wrists. He was tying her up!

Her breath caught somewhere in her throat. A flicker of traitorous excitement rushed through her body, spurting through her veins like champagne bubbling up out of the bottle. She suppressed it, determined not to give in to him. "Nick! Stop! Don't you dare do this to me!"

But he already had. Her wrists were securely bound. He straddled her, lifting her a little, and dragged her up the bed so that he could fasten the other end of the tie to the headboard. And then he sat there, a knee on either side of her body, his hands on his lean hips, and stared down at her like a warrior with his prize.

He was panting himself now, a gleam of excitement in his hot-coffee eyes, a flush coloring his chiseled face, a light sweat already shimmering across his broad shoulders and powerful chest. She could feel him, hard, against her stomach.

Excitement, hot and breathless, coursed through her. She felt deliciously helpless, stretched out beneath him with her hands tied, voluptuously sensual with her back bowed to present her breasts for his inspection, desirable beyond belief or imagination.

He reached out, cupping her breasts in his palms, and placed his thumbs over the hardened nipples.

Samantha moaned. "Nick, dammit." She pulled weakly against her bonds, arching her back even more. "If you don't untie me right this minute I'll . . . I'll . . ."

"You'll what?" he said silkily, his eyes hot and greedy.

"I'll *bite* you," she purred.

His nostrils flared. "So bite," he invited.

He leaned forward and touched his open mouth to her throat again. And then he trailed his lips over all of the sensitive little hollows along her elegant collarbone, following a straining tendon upward to the delicate curve of her ear, deliberately placing his shoulder within easy reach of her teeth.

Samantha lifted her head from the bed and opened her mouth over his flesh but she didn't bite him. She nibbled. Gently. Her tongue snaked out, tasting him, making wet circles all along the broad expanse of his shoulder to where it curved into his neck, covering the place where his pulse pounded with a strong, steady beat. Then she bit him. Hard.

He groaned against her neck. "Bitch," he said, but the word was a caress.

He slid down her body, pressing his open mouth all over her fragile upper chest before sliding his tongue to the shallow valley between her breasts. He moved his head from side to side, his cupped hands pushing the soft globes higher as his tongue flicked first one nipple and then the other. Samantha arched against his mouth, her body begging for a firmer pressure.

But he left her wanting, her breasts aching, and moved farther down, his thumbs rotating against her nipples, his lips scattering soft, sweet, hot kisses along her narrow midriff and the flatness of her stomach.

Samantha began to quiver in breathless anticipation, every nerve in her body screaming for more. She felt his tongue dart into the depression of her navel for a too-brief second, and then his hands left her breasts, sliding down over the inward-sloping curve of her waist and the gentle flare of her hips to the inside of her thighs. He pushed them apart, opening her for the most intimate kiss of all.

Samantha's back arched off the bed when his mouth touched her. She clenched her teeth against the shriek that rose to her lips, turning it into a soft, wordless wail of mindless ecstasy. Her fingers opened and closed spasmodically, clutching at the silken bonds that held her, relishing and railing against the way they somehow intensified the feeling that gripped her.

She wanted to reach out and hold him, touch him, give back to him just a measure of the pleasure that he was so unselfishly giving to her but she couldn't. All she could do was feel; wallowing shamelessly, guiltlessly, gloriously, in hedonistic sensuality, while he devoured her like a gourmand at an epicurean feast.

The feeling inside her built and built, climbing ever higher, hotter, hurting almost, until it finally boiled over into almost unbearable pleasure. Every long, lean muscle in her body tightened as she exploded into an ecstasy more intense, more fulfilling than anything she'd ever experienced before.

Nick lay still for a minute or two, his face pressed into the softness of her quivering stomach, listening to her little gasping breaths and the way she chanted his name over and over without seeming to be aware of it. His heart felt as if it were about to explode, his body raged to be inside her, his starving soul longed to hear the words of love he hadn't let her say.

"Nick." She was almost sobbing. Her hips undulated against him. "Nick, please."

He surged upward, entering her with a controlled thrust of male power, feeling the incredible warmth and softness of her in every fiber of his body. She wrapped her legs around him, holding him in the only way she could.

"It's good," he groaned. His hips were tight against hers, pressed deep, savoring the feeling. "So good."

"Untie me," she whispered. "I want to hold you, too. Untie me."

He reached up, fumbling for the tie, and managed to loosen it from the headboard. Without waiting for him to free her wrists, Samantha brought her hands over his head. "Now," she commanded, holding him as tightly as she could. "Now, Nick."

He began to move against her with long, slow thrusts designed to prolong the feeling for as long as humanly possible. But the feeling itself defeated him, and he had no choice but to move faster, harder, driving her, and himself, ever closer to the edge.

Samantha matched him thrust for thrust, and together they experienced the feeling to the breaking point, coiling muscle and sinew and emotions ever tighter until they sprang loose, spinning off into a space where the only reality was each other.

"I love you, Nick," she said fiercely, softly, clutching him to her as the feeling overwhelmed her control. "I love you."

"I know." He cradled her close, brushing at her hair, kissing her flushed cheeks, shaken to the very core by the need to say the words back to her. Years of habit and caution held him back, and the unconscious, deep-seated fear of what abandoning oneself to love could do to a person. "I know you do," he whispered, giving her the only words he could.

Miraculously, they seemed to satisfy her. She stopped clutching at him and tucked her head into the curve of his neck, nestling against him.

Nick kissed her temple and then reared back a little to look at her face. A tender smile curved his lips. "Still think you'll never speak to me again?" he teased, reminding her of the threat she'd made.

Samantha stared at him blankly for a moment.

He reached behind his neck and grasped one end of the tie that still wrapped her wrists. One good tug pulled it loose. He tossed it aside.

Samantha giggled. "You pervert."

"Maybe." He rolled over, bringing her on top of him. "But you enjoyed it as much as I did."

"Pervert," she accused again. Blushing, she kissed his chest, then tenderly placed her cheek against the place she'd kissed. "But I like it."

Nick hugged her fiercely. "I'm glad," he said against the top of her head.

She felt his lips move in a brief kiss against her hair, and then his arms loosened and he began stroking the curve of her back. Long, idle caresses that gradually slowed, then stopped as his breathing deepened and he fell asleep.

Samantha lay quietly, her cheek pressed against his chest, listening to his heart beating under her ear, her mind in too much of a turmoil to sleep. Too awhirl with the endless possibilities that his tender words and loving actions implied. Tormented, too, by a steadily building guilt.

She *hated* lying to the man she'd fallen in love with. Fallen unmistakably, irrevocably in love with. In the face of what they'd just shared, her deception seemed far worse than it might otherwise have been. She wanted, desperately, to tell him everything, to lay it all before him and erase the lie between them. But she couldn't. She'd promised Robbie.

Would Nick understand a lie told out of loyalty and familial love?

She raised her head cautiously and stared down into his sleeping face. He looked less formidable asleep, she thought, less resolute and overpoweringly male. More endearingly vulnerable. She touched the corner of his mouth lightly, lovingly, reminded of the old newspaper photo her mother had sent her. All of his vulnerability was here, in his beautiful chiseled lips, she thought. It had showed in the newspaper photo. It showed now, while he slept.

Samantha felt a surge of tenderness, protective and nurturing, rise up in her. For all his strength, he could be hurt. Her love for him seemed suddenly sweeter. And infinitely more fragile.

Damn Robbie for putting me in this position! she thought, surprising herself with her own vehemence.

But it wasn't really Robbie's fault, she thought then, still staring blindly into Nick's sleeping face. It wasn't anybody's fault, really.

Nick's dark lashes fluttered as if he were disturbed by her unwavering stare. He opened his eyes. "What are you thinking about?" he murmured, wondering why she looked so pensive.

"You," she whispered. She inched herself up slightly to touch her lips briefly to his. "Just you."

But it was another lie. Or, rather, not the whole truth. She sighed and rolled sideways off him and swung her feet to the floor.

"Don't let it go to your head, though," she said teasingly, glancing at him over her bare shoulder. "I say that to all the guys."

He reached for her, as she knew he would, but she was quicker. She jumped up from the bed, well out of his reach, and bent to retrieve her panties and bra from the floor.

"No more of that, you pervert," she told him sternly, stepping into her underpants while he watched her from the bed. "Come on, get up," she commanded when he folded his arms under his head. "I want to do *some* sight-seeing while I'm in Paris."

"You'll see Paris tonight," he reminded her lazily, not moving. He felt incredibly content and comfortable, lying there, watching her wriggle into her clothes.

"No, I won't," she said from beneath the scarlet folds of her oversized sweater.

Nick considered pulling her down to the bed for another bout of lovemaking. Long, lazy, tender lovemaking to suit his mood.

Samantha's head appeared through the neck of the sweater. "I'll be working tonight. Remember?" She smoothed down the front of the sweater, then lifted both hands and ran her fingers through her tangled hair. "Do you have a brush? A comb, even? Oh, no wait." She spied her leather shoulder bag on the floor near her leather pants. "I've got one." She scooped up the pants and bag and headed for the bathroom.

"Do you really want to go sight-seeing?" Nick asked from the bed. Her legs were long and smooth—the palest ivory against the bright red sweater that brushed her thighs.

Samantha turned in the bathroom doorway to look at him. "Yes, I really want to go sight-seeing."

He patted the empty space next to him on the bed. "Sure I couldn't change your mind?"

No, she wasn't sure. He looked so magnificent lying there, his strong, hair-dusted body bronze against the wine-colored sheets, his grin inviting, his dark eyes full of tenderness and amusement and the beginnings of renewed lust. She felt her stomach knot. If she went back to bed with him now, she'd end up telling him how much she loved him again. And he wasn't quite ready for that. She'd also probably end up telling him all about Robbie, too.

Well, would that be so bad? asked a little voice inside her.

She considered the idea for about two seconds. Yes, it would be bad. For Robbie. He had enough problems right now, feeling insecure and inadequate, worrying about his talent, doubting his creativity. She couldn't add the threat of losing his job to all of that.

She shook her head at Nick, backing into the bathroom as she spoke. "Yes, I'm sure," she lied. "Now get up, you sex fiend. I want to see more of Paris than just the ceiling of this hotel room."

7

"OH, NICK, this is beautiful." Samantha leaned farther forward in her seat as the long black car turned into an open iron gate that was set into the high stone wall running along the narrow road. Well-tended lawns bordered a driveway of crushed white rock. Heavily laden climbing rose vines clung to the rustic wall of a low, sprawling villa, their blossoms brilliant against the soft rose of the building. Faded red shutters matched the tiled roof. "You forgot to mention that it was a Renaissance mansion." She slanted an amused glance at him. There were so many things he hadn't told her. "The old family homestead, I think you said."

Nick let out a breath he hadn't even known he'd been holding. "Hardly a mansion," he said. The villa dated from the late nineteenth century, a bit worn now, a bit faded but still charming to those who cared to look. He was glad she had.

"How long has it been in the family?" Samantha asked as the car's tires crunched over the gravel driveway.

"Eighty years or so, in a manner of speaking."

"In a manner of speaking?"

"My grandfather was a servant here at one time. Something like an English butler. My father would have followed in his footsteps if he hadn't emigrated to

America." He broke off as the car came to a stop, reaching out to open the door before the driver could get out and do it for him.

He stood still for a moment, savoring the sights and smells of his homecoming, and then turned and helped Samantha from the back seat with a hand under her elbow. After giving the driver a few pleasant instructions in flawless Italian he led her up the wide, worn steps to the heavy, double-wide front door. It was painted a faded red, like the shutters, and had a single rose intricately carved into each center panel.

"So how did you end up owning it?" Samantha said, reaching out to touch the outline of one of the roses. It matched the one engraved on the gold cuff links Nick always wore. She smiled at him over her shoulder. "Or should I say when?"

Nick's eyes glinted, returning her smile. "About six years ago. I'd taken some time off after I finished college. The family business was doing fairly well by then—we were out of the red, anyway—and I decided to take a vacation." He gave her a wry grin. "Search out my roots, so to speak. My Aunt Aida had never left Italy and was still a servant here. The cook. Good cook, too. You'll love her scampi. Anyway, when the opportunity came to buy it, I did. It seemed like the right thing to do at the time."

"Poetic justice?"

"Something like that, I guess." He shrugged but Samantha knew instinctively that the acquisition of the home where his grandfather had been a servant was important to him. "I only wish my father had been alive to see it," he said, confirming her thought. "Well," he cupped her elbow again. "Shall we go in?"

The front hall was a few degrees cooler than the outside. The ceiling was low and beamed, the walls were white stucco, the terra cotta tiles on the floor were polished to a high sheen. A rococo sideboard, extravagantly carved, sat against one wall with a gold-framed mirror above it and a huge vase of lush red roses sitting atop its gleaming surface. A large oil painting, looking suspiciously like an original Botticelli, graced the wall between two arched doorways.

Entranced, Samantha wandered over to take a closer look at it just as a young girl came flying through one of the open archways. Samantha received a quick impression of long legs, a brief red shorts set and a mane of dark, curly hair.

"Nick!" the girl cried and launched herself into his arms. She was swallowed up in an enthusiastic hug that lifted her bare feet off the floor.

"Marina." Nick kissed both cheeks soundly before putting her down. He surveyed her somewhat anxiously, his dark eyes raking over her upturned face. "How are you?"

"I'm fine. Feeling much better." One small hand came up to caress his lean cheek. "Really."

"You look wonderful." He held her a little away from him, his hands huge against her thin shoulders. "You've even gained some weight, I think," he said approvingly. "And a tan."

The girl smiled. "A little."

"That's good." He kissed her again and then hugged her to his side, one arm draped around her shoulders.

"Samantha, I'd like you to meet my youngest sister, Marina. Marina, this is Samantha Spencer."

"Oh, yes." Her smile was beautiful, like Nick's, but a bit shy. "I know who you are." She glanced fondly up at her brother. "Nick sent me some pictures of his Sophisticated Lady. I'm very glad to meet you." She held out a thin hand.

Not a young girl, Samantha thought, taking it, but a young woman. She was at least twenty, not the fifteen that Samantha had at first supposed. She looked as if she'd been quite ill and was just starting to recover. Her dark hair was thick and curly but just a little dull. Her eyes—so like Nick's—were ringed with faint shadows.

"I'm very glad to meet you, too," Samantha said. "Nick didn't tell me he had a sister living in Italy. I just assumed that all of his family lived in New York."

"Oh, I do . . . I was. I mean . . ." She lifted her eyes to Nick's face.

"Marina's on a little vacation at the moment. She's been ill," Nick answered for his sister.

Was it her imagination, Samantha wondered, or had he actually hesitated over the last word? "Yes, of course. I read something about you being ill in the paper. And recuperating in Italy, too. I should have remembered."

"Marina, honey, where's Aunt Aida?"

"Oh." Marina recovered her lovely smile. "That's what I came to tell you. *Zia* Aida is out on the terrace. She's putting the finishing touches on the luncheon table." Marina turned her smile on Samantha. "I hope you're hungry. She's gone all out."

"Starving," Samantha assured her, ignoring Nick's teasing grin.

"Please, come on out then. The terrace is beautiful this time of day and *Zia* Aida has used the rose table linen and all her best china. It's very pretty. Or..." she hesitated, giving Nick that little lost girl look again. "Maybe...maybe you'd like to freshen up first?" She seemed on the verge of tears suddenly. "I should have thought of that first, I guess. You've had a long trip. I'm sorry, I should have—"

"I don't need to freshen up first, thanks." Samantha linked her arm through Marina's, earning herself a warm look of approval from Nick as he took his sister's other arm. "Which way to the terrace? I'm starved."

A matronly woman, small and a bit plump, hurried toward them as they came out onto the stone terrace. She wore a plain black dress with a lace collar, opaque black stockings and sturdy black shoes. Her hair was arranged into a fat bun low on the back of her head. Her lined face was split into a wide, welcoming smile.

Nick's smile again, Samantha thought. The family resemblance was very strong.

"*Bentornato*, Nick!" she said warmly, pulling his face down to hers so that she could kiss his cheeks. "*Bentornato!*" She kissed him again. "Welcome home." She switched to heavily accented English for the benefit of their guest. "It has been *quanto tempo*—a long time?—since you have been home."

"*Si, Zia* Aida." He nodded, returning her affectionate greeting with a kiss of his own. "Too long. *Come sta?*" he asked.

"Bene. Molto bene. E tu?"

"Bene. A little tired. It's been a long trip." He grinned suddenly at Samantha as if to imply that it hadn't been the trip that was sapping his strength. "But very well."

Aida's sharp black eyes caught the look he sent to the tall, fair-haired woman beside him and she smiled slyly, winking, and said something to him in rapid Italian. Nick laughed and shook his head, grinning all the while.

It didn't take a linguistics expert to get the general drift of what was being said. Samantha felt the beginnings of a blush creeping up to color her cheeks. Aida crowed with delighted laughter and launched into another spate of unintelligible questions.

"Si, si, Zia Aida. She's very beautiful but, no, she isn't my *fidanzata."*

Samantha recognized the word from some movie she'd seen. It meant *fiancée.*

"She's Nick's Sophisticated Lady, *Zia* Aida," Marina said. "You know, for the new Gavino Cosmetics division. *Cosmetico,"* she translated for her aunt. "Miss Spencer is a model. *Modella."*

"Ah, *si. Modella."* Aida nodded her understanding. She turned to Samantha. *"Sono molto lieto de far la sua conoscenza, Signorina,"* she said graciously, grasping one of Samantha's hands in both of hers.

Samantha realized she was being welcomed but she wasn't quite sure how to respond. Her eyes sought Nick's.

He reached out, placing an arm around her slim shoulders, and drew her close to his side. *"Zia* Aida says she is very pleased to meet you."

"Si, very pleased," echoed the older woman. She squeezed Samantha's hand again, a wide smile on her face. "You are most welcome, *Signorina* Spencer."

"Grazie." Samantha used the only Italian word she knew and returned the friendly pressure of the other woman's hands. "But, please, call me Samantha."

"Si, Samantha," she said, giving it a charming Italian pronunciation. "And I am *Zia* Aida. Now you will come and eat, *si?"*

"Si," said Nick, chuckling. "You don't have to invite Samantha twice, not when there's food involved."

Aida herded them all over to one of the four umbrella tables that dotted the length of the stone terrace. The rose-colored linen that Marina had mentioned almost exactly matched the faded red tiles of the low, sloping roof. The flowers that decorated the table were obviously from the sweet-smelling roses that climbed all along the low stone wall of the terrace and the more formal rose garden beyond. A garden which continued in splendidly gaudy profusion all the way down a slight incline to the smooth, manicured lawn and a mosaic-tiled swimming pool, sparkling blue and inviting in the warm Italian sunlight.

"You can see now why the house is called the Villa Rosa," Nick said, smiling across the table at Samantha when she brought her attention back to him.

She returned his smile warmly. "This is marvelous, *Zia* Aida," she said expansively. Her glance roved over the beautifully set table. "It all looks so delicious. And I'm—"

"—Starved," Samantha and Nick finished together.

"Do you not feed her?" Aida scolded Nick in her charming, broken English. She looked puzzled when both Nick and Samantha burst into laughter but she was quite willing to join in, even if she didn't understand why.

"All the time, *Zia* Aida," Nick assured his aunt. "All the time."

"Well, she does not look as if she is well fed."

"Models aren't supposed to look well fed," said Marina. "They're supposed to be thin."

"*Si*? This is true?" She looked at Samantha for confirmation.

"Very true," Samantha nodded, lifting her spoon to taste what Aida had placed in front of her. It looked like a mixture of rice and peas with bits of chicken in some sort of soup base. "The thinner, the better."

Aida looked askance at her nephew. "You do not want her to be—" The correct English word failed her but she moved her hands in a universally known gesture, describing a very voluptuous hourglass figure in the air.

Nick laughed, more at ease than Samantha had ever seen him, and shook his head. "Samantha is plenty, ah, well-rounded enough for me," he said, casting a warm look in her direction.

Samantha lowered her eyes. "This soup is delicious, *Zia* Aida."

"Samantha likes authentic food," Nick said.

"What do you call it?" Samantha asked, ignoring him.

"It is *risi e bisi*. Made in the spring only. With fresh peas."

"And this?" Samantha asked, forking up a mouthful of delicate sole in some sort of herb sauce.

"*Sfogie in saor,*" Aida told her, heartily approving of Samantha's healthy appetite.

They talked pleasantly, if a little desultorily, all during the rest of the meal. Nick entertained Marina and his aunt with stories about the crew of the *Sophisticated Lady* campaign, explaining again that they had miraculously managed to finish ahead of schedule in Paris and, so, had all gained a day to do as they pleased as a reward for their hard work. He had decided to bring Samantha to the Villa Rosa as his reward, he said, smiling at her across the rose-covered table.

Samantha smiled back, content to sit and listen and watch. She tasted everything put in front of her, enjoying it all and complimenting Aida extravagantly but with obvious sincerity. She noticed, without seeming to, that Marina barely picked at her food, pushing it around on her plate instead of eating it.

The poor girl must have been really ill, she thought, wondering what had been—or still was—the matter with her. She'd ask Nick later, she decided, stifling a yawn behind one hand.

"You are *assonnata*—sleepy?" Aida's voice claimed her wandering attention.

Samantha smiled. "A little, I guess. It's been a long day already. And all of this—" she waved a graceful hand, indicating the beautiful, peaceful surroundings, the warm sun, the steady hum of the bees flitting through the rose bushes "—has made me awfully lazy. Besides," she patted her stomach. "A delicious meal like this always makes me sleepy."

"Then you must take a rest." Aida rose to her feet. "Marina will show you to your room."

"Really, it's not necessary. I can relax right here." She tilted her head back against her chair and closed her eyes against the sun. "It's so peaceful."

"*Si*, peaceful," agreed Aida as she began gathering up plates. "But you go. Marina will show you." She smiled at her nephew. "Nick will have another small glass of *grappa* and then he, too, will take a rest. It is good to rest in the afternoon." She waved the two younger women away. "Go now."

They went.

"*Zia* Aida wants to talk to Nick," Marina told her as they strolled down the long, tiled hallway. It was lined with lovely old portraits and polished shields and groupings of richly decorated antique weapons. "About me," she added, looking sideways at Samantha to judge the effect of her words.

Samantha nodded. "I could tell that you'd been ill," she said gently. Marina seemed to require gentleness. "But you look like you're on the road to recovery."

"I am." Marina gave a heartfelt sigh. "Thanks to Nick. If it hadn't been for him, I don't know what would have happened to me." Her eyes clouded up for a moment. "I'd probably be dead now, I guess." She shook her head, the dark hair just skimming her bare shoulders, and brushed at her eyes with the back of one hand. "I'm sorry. Nick tells me not to think about it too much." She smiled a little shakily at Samantha. "I try not to. But sometimes it's so hard, I...well, never mind. You don't want to hear my problems."

"Sometimes it helps to talk about them," Samantha offered.

"Oh, I've *talked* about them. Nick sent me to a shrink before I came here, but it didn't seem to do much good." She shrugged and smiled, dismissing the thought. "Not like being here has. Helped, I mean." She pushed open one of the doors leading off the hall. "Nick said that you were to have this room."

It was decorated in soft yellow and robin's egg blue with white-washed walls and heavy pieces of beautifully carved, old-fashioned wood furniture. Sheer pale yellow curtains hung at the windows, bracketed by heavier drapes in a blue and yellow flower pattern reminiscent of a medieval tapestry. A matching bedspread covered the massive four-poster bed.

"That's the bathroom," Marina said, pointing to the other door in the room. "It connects with Nick's room," she said, watching Samantha's face for a reaction.

"Oh," was all Samantha could think of to say. If this was Nick's way of letting his family know there was a relationship between them, she would have preferred something less ambiguous, like an outright statement of his feelings. But this was, hopefully, a start.

Marina sat down on the edge of the big baroque four-poster bed that dominated the room and crossed her bare legs under her. "Are you in love with my brother?" She peered at Samantha, her eyes shadowed with some not-yet-forgotten pain.

She hesitated, wondering why Marina would ask such a personal question of someone she'd just met. "Yes, I am," she said honestly, seeing no need to hide her own feelings. She had, after all, already told Nick how she felt. "I love him very much."

Marina uncoiled her legs and stood up. "That's good," she said, moving toward Samantha. "You're very beautiful and Nick likes beautiful women. You're sweet, too, I can tell. And patient, I think. And you have laughing eyes. Nick needs someone to make him laugh. Lord knows, none of us seem to be able to make him laugh very often, except *Zia* Aida. And she likes you." She stopped directly in front of Samantha and gave her a long considering look. She went up on tiptoes, touching her cheek to the taller woman's. "I like you, too," she said softly. And then she left, quietly closing the bedroom door behind her.

Now what was that all about?

Samantha shook her head. There was such an air of fragility about Nick's sister. She was like a delicate china doll that had been dropped and painstakingly glued back together. Samantha felt as if the girl might fall apart at the slightest wrong word. Or even a too-hard stare, Samantha thought, turning to look for her suitcases.

They weren't in plain sight. She crossed the room to the massive armoire that took up nearly half of one whole wall, thinking absently that the pale yellow, rose-strewn carpet beneath her feet should be hanging on a museum wall somewhere instead of covering a floor for people to walk on.

Her clothes had been hung neatly in the armoire, the unpacked suitcases on the shelf above them. She should have realized that a house this size would have servants, even if Aida Gavino still did her own cooking.

Undressing quickly, Samantha slipped into the white cashmere robe that she'd first worn in Paris and went into the bathroom.

It was a huge room, obviously converted to its present use. The walls were washed in yellow; so pale that it appeared that the color was only a reflection of the sunlight that streamed in from the open windows set high in the wall. Deeper golden-yellow tiles, interspersed with ones of clear ocean blue, formed a complicated pattern along the edge of the ceiling and the floor and around each of the two doors. There were two deep shell-shaped sinks set into a counter of the same blue and gold tiles, and a huge tub, with two steps up to it, that could have quite easily held four people. To call it opulent would be a gross understatement.

Samantha decided against taking a shower, since it would mean wetting her hair, and settled for a thorough wash in one of the shell-shaped sinks. She scrubbed her face clean of makeup, cleaned her teeth and brushed out her hair. Feeling refreshed and just the tiniest bit guilty for having messed up the pristine perfection of the bathroom, she returned to the bedroom.

Someone had been in the room again. The bed was turned down to reveal crisp white sheets edged with an eyelet ruffle. The long windows had been opened, letting in a warm, rose-scented breeze that fluttered the sheer curtains. It was disconcerting to have someone creeping in and out of your bedroom, Samantha thought, like some sort of magic genie. It would also be incredibly easy to get used to.

Yawning, she dropped her robe across the foot of the huge bed and slipped, naked, into the inviting coolness of the crisp sheets. They were rose scented, too, she realized, just before sleep took her.

8

SHE WAS STILL SLEEPING when Nick entered her bedroom through the connecting bathroom. She lay on her side, facing away from him, her shoulders bared above the ruffled hem of the sheet. A rounded knee and the pink-nailed toes of one foot peeked out from under the lower edge. Nick stood at the end of the massive four-poster bed, watching her sleep, wondering what it was about her that threatened to get through all of his carefully erected defenses.

She was a beautiful woman. She was elegant and charming. She was also... His brow wrinkled as he puzzled over exactly the right word. Sweet? Oh, God, yes, deliciously sweet! Innocent and provocative, playful and teasing, warm and open and giving. So giving.

His hand tightened on the bedpost.

Easily, effortlessly, with just her sweet smile and a look that was anything but cool, she had him thinking about things he knew from experience were impossible. Love. Marriage. Forever after. Fairy tales.

She even looked as if she belonged in a fairy tale, he thought. Like a princess with smooth, gleaming skin and silvery hair, waiting for her prince to awaken her with a kiss. Unable to resist, Nick sat down on the edge of the bed and leaned over her, brushing her tumbled hair aside with a gentle hand.

"Wake up, Sleeping Beauty," he mumbled into the soft, warm flesh of her nape. She smelled of roses and dreams.

She rolled over. "Nick," she said and smiled up at him. "Have I been asleep long?"

"Most of the afternoon." He brushed back a lock of her hair, smoothing it against the eyelet pillow. "You must have been exhausted."

"Just disgustingly lazy." She reached up and touched his cheek. "Did you get a chance to take a nap, too?"

Nick turned his lips into her hand. "I outgrew naps when I was five years old," he said against her palm.

Her fingers moved upward, smoothing through the hair at his temple. "Well, you look rested," she said, her eyes roving over him.

He had shed his jacket and tie. The top few buttons of his white shirt were undone and the sleeves were rolled partway up, revealing the light covering of dark hair on his wrists and brawny forearms. A healthy flush of new color touched his cheeks and forehead and nose.

"And relaxed," she added. She dropped her hand to his shoulder, absently rubbing the rounded muscle with her open palm. "Are you sure you didn't take a nap?"

"I may have dozed a bit in the sun," he admitted, curbing the desire to lean into her caressing hand like a cat demanding more. He drew back a little. "Why don't you haul yourself out of there," he suggested, "and come on outside and get a little sun, yourself, before dinner."

Samantha shook her head against the pillow. "I burn." Her hand trailed down his shoulder to the bare skin of his forearm. It was warm and hard against her palm; the tiny hairs were silky soft. Her smile deepened into provocation. "Why don't you haul yourself in here instead and get some—" her fingers tip-toed down to his hand where it rested on the pillow beside her head "—rest," she said, looking up at him from beneath half-lowered lashes.

Nick grinned. "None of that now. *Zia* Aida knows I'm in here," he admonished. "She sent me." But he lowered his head, nonetheless, burying his face in the tender curve of her throat. He braced his hands on either side of her head, using his chin to nuzzle the sheet lower.

She felt his warm breath in the valley between her breasts. His hair brushed against the underside of her chin. She lifted her arms, wrapping them around his neck, and pulled him down to cradle him close against her heart.

Nick sighed. "I'm supposed to be finding out what you want for dinner," he said against her breast. Her scent was all around him, sweet and soft and comforting. "So, what do you want for dinner?"

"You," she whispered into his ear.

"Is that all you ever think about?" He tried to sound disapproving but his voice was warm with pleasure, and his arms held her tight.

"All I ever think about," she agreed, moving invitingly against him. "Well?" She put her hands on either side of his face and lifted his head so she could look into his eyes. "Do I get you?"

Yes, he wanted to say. *Yes, you get me. For always. Forever. Till death do us part*. But the words seemed to stick in his throat.

"Yes, you'll get me, you hussy," he said, answering her question at a level he could handle. "And I'll get you. But not right now. *Zia* Aida is probably waiting right outside the door, counting the minutes that I'm in here."

Samantha stuck her bottom lip out. "If you'd hurry, it wouldn't take more than a few minutes."

Nick grinned wickedly. "The way I feel right now, it'd take a hell of a lot more than a few minutes." He leaned down to brush a quick, butterfly kiss over her pouting mouth. Her lips opened immediately under his, warm and giving. Always giving, inviting him to stay and take.

He sighed and sat up. "Tell you what." He touched a finger to her lips, trailing it down her chin and throat and chest to the valley between her breasts. "Why don't I tell *Zia* Aida that we'll be going out for dinner?" He circled one breast and then the other. "We could drive down into town and have dinner at the Ristorante Al Santo. Just the two of us." He cupped one small mound in his palm. "Would you like that?"

"Yes." Samantha's voice was soft and breathless. "If it wouldn't upset your aunt, I'd like that very much."

"So would I." He leaned down again, and placed a soft kiss on the peak of the captured breast, and then another on her parted lips. "You get up and get dressed. Nothing too fancy." He stood up. "I'll go tell *Zia* Aida that we won't be here for dinner."

Samantha sat up, unconcerned that the sheet fell away from her upper body. "She won't be upset, will she? I mean, it's your first night home and everything. And there's Marina." Fragile Marina with the haunted eyes needed careful, considerate handling. "She probably wants to spend some time with you, too."

"Marina and I spent most of the afternoon together. She's already gone to bed. She still tires very easily," he explained.

"Then *Zia* Aida will be eating alone."

Nick shook his head. "In the kitchen with Rosina and Salvatore, the live-in staff. *Dallas* is on TV tonight. She won't even know we're gone." He cast one last, lingering look at her and then turned toward the bedroom door. "You've got thirty minutes to get ready."

Samantha jumped up before the door had closed behind him, heading for the bathroom. Twenty minutes later she was standing in front of the mirror at the old-fashioned dressing table, putting the finishing touches to her ensemble. She'd settled on a softly gathered, mid-calf skirt in hot pink cotton gauze with a turquoise tank top tucked into it and the matching pink short-sleeved shirt worn open as a light jacket. Her narrow waist was wrapped with a wide woven leather belt. She wore flat-heeled, leather sandals with thin straps that tied around her trim ankles, an armful of silver bangle bracelets and big silver hoops in her pierced ears. She was bent over from the waist, vigorously brushing her hair, when a light knock sounded on the door.

"Yes?" she hollered.

Nick's dark head appeared around the edge. "Ready?" he asked, his eyes gleaming appreciatively as she straightened and tossed her mane of hair back with a quick shake of her head.

"Ready." She snatched up her purse as she passed the bed and slung it over her shoulder, then held out her hand to Nick as she crossed to the door. "Was your aunt upset when you told her that we wouldn't be eating with her?"

"Not at all." Nick tucked her hand into the crook of his elbow as they ambled down the hall. "She was very pleased that you were concerned about it, though. Said it shows what a well-brought-up young woman you are." He grinned. "Shows you how little she knows, doesn't it?" he said outrageously, his deliberately leering expression leaving no doubt as to what he meant.

Samantha lifted her chin with pretend hauteur. "I'm very well brought up," she said imperiously and then spoiled the affect with a throaty chuckle. "I hope you didn't disillusion her about my character," she chided him.

"Far be it from me to sully my aunt's ears with—"

Samantha punched him in the arm before he could finish.

Laughing, Nick grabbed her fist in his hand before she could land a second punch and propelled her through the foyer and out onto the sun-warmed front steps.

"Think you can ride this in that skirt?"

"*This*" was a baby blue Vespa. Nick swung one long, jeans-clad leg across the vinyl saddle and looked back over his shoulder, his expression inviting her to climb on behind him. Gathering her skirt around her legs, she did.

"I've never ridden a motorcycle before," she said, tucking the skirt up under her legs. "But I've always wanted to."

"I wouldn't call this a motorcycle. It's more like a moped." He started the engine. "All settled?"

Samantha nodded, her cheek rubbing against the deep red knit shirt that covered his back.

He patted her hands, pulling them tighter around his waist. "Hold on."

The Vespa sprang to life, surging forward with a quick spurt of power. In minutes they'd navigated the gravel drive of the Villa Rosa and were winding down the road to the town of Padua.

Samantha buried her face against Nick's back for the first few minutes, getting used to the sensation of flying over the ground. She could feel the wind carrying her hair out behind her. It tugged at the edges of her tucked up skirt and billowed the loose, open shirt she wore.

"This is terrific," she hollered, lifting her head. "How fast are we going?"

He tapped the speedometer. Samantha pushed her hair out of her face and peered over his shoulder.

"Thirty-five? Is that all?" It felt as if they were going much faster as they zig-zagged along the narrow road. "I thought sixty, at least."

The wind carried Nick's deep laugh back to her and she felt his stomach muscles contract beneath her encircling arms. Marina's words came back to her. *Nick needs someone to make him laugh. Lord knows, none of us seem to be able to make him laugh very often.* Well, *she* could make him laugh. She tightened her arms around his lean waist and rubbed her cheek against his shoulder, loving him, at that precise moment, with every fiber of her being.

His muscles flexed under her cheek. "There," he said, lifting one hand from the controls of the Vespa to point. "Do you see it? Wait, it'll be around the next curve. There." He steered the Vespa to the side of the narrow road, killing the engine, and pointed in a south-easterly direction. Samantha could see a glimmer of blue shimmering in the last long rays of the setting sun.

"The Mediterranean?" she guessed.

"The Adriatic Sea," he corrected her, "or, to be even more precise, the Gulf of Venice. You'll be down there in a couple of days, floating on a gondola through the Great Canal of Venice. How does that sound?"

"Wonderful." She squeezed his middle. "As long as you're there, too."

Nick stilled in her arms. "I wish you wouldn't say things like that," he said, very quietly. "It makes me—"

"Makes you what?" she said softly.

"Makes me want—" he shrugged uneasily "—things."

"What things?"

He turned to look over his shoulder at her and Samantha saw the burning light in his eyes. She recognized it for what it was, even if he didn't yet. The beginnings of joy flooded through her.

"What things?" she said again.

"Things." He paused, hovering on the edge, and then plunged over. "You."

The moment he said it, she felt him withdraw. "Well, that's easy enough," she said lightly. "You have me, any time you want me."

Nick twisted completely around in the Vespa saddle, one hand lifting to cup her cheek, and kissed her. Hard. "Later," he promised.

He gunned the Vespa to life again and they took off down the road, winding through the rugged beauty of the Italian foothills into town. It was dusk as they entered Padua but the narrow, cobbled streets were full of life. Samantha craned her neck, trying to see everything there was to see.

The houses were close together, most sharing a common wall. Some had been left unpainted and had weathered to a gentle, beaten gray, others were whitewashed, and still others were painted a soft, faded rose like the Villa Rosa.

Old women, dressed in black like *Zia* Aida, sat gossiping on their front steps, enjoying the soft, evening air while they kept an eagle eye on the darting children who were playing one last game before it was time to go in.

Young people, in their teens and twenties, were dressed in the same jeans and T-shirts and casual sports clothes worn by young people the world over. There were older men in business suits or laborer's overalls and women in print dresses on the way home from the market.

Bicycles were everywhere. Motor scooters like the Vespa put-putted through the crowded streets. An occasional car braved the narrow passageways. All of them somehow managed to avoid crashing into either the pedestrians or each other.

"It's a lovely town," Samantha said as Nick pulled up next to a metal bicycle rack. She dismounted, standing to one side while he padlocked the Vespa to the rack. "Just like New York," she quipped as he straightened.

"Except that it'll still be here when we get back." He reached for her hand, leading her through a wide archway, and then stood back, watching her as she took it all in.

"Oh, Nick!" Wide-eyed with delight, she made a slow circle in the middle of the piazza, scattering pigeons with the flaring hem of her pink skirt and the oversized shoulder bag that dangled from her fingers.

How had he ever thought she was another one of those same worldly, sophisticated women he'd known before? He must have been blind, he thought. Or crazy. Samantha was no more like the Sophisticated Lady she portrayed than a wildflower was like a painted porcelain rose.

"It looks just like something out of *Roman Holiday*," she said. "With Audrey Hepburn, remember? She played a princess who ran away and fell in love with Gregory Peck."

"I hope this doesn't mean you're going to run off and get your hair cut."

Samantha's hand went to her head. "That's right. She did do that in the movie, didn't she?" She pushed her hair up with both hands, her purse dangling from the crook of her elbow. "How do you think I'd look with a pixie haircut?"

"Like a tall pixie." He looped his arm over her shoulders, pulling her close to his side. "But don't try it," he growled in her ear. "Cut one strand of your hair and I'll beat you black and blue."

"Chauvinist."

"You better believe it." He squeezed her shoulders. "But you like it."

"A conceited chauvinist, at that. Must be the Italian in you."

"Probably," he admitted complacently.

Samantha laughed in pure delight and slipped her arm around his lean waist. "Tell me about this place. What's it called?"

"You are in Padua, Italy," he began in a deep, professorial voice, "on the continent of Europe."

She gave him an exasperated look. "I know *that*. Tell me something else."

"You didn't know when you were looking at the Adriatic Sea," he reminded her.

She shrugged. "Minor point."

"Not to an Italian. Okay, okay." He fended off a pretend blow. "Padua is also known as *La Citta del Santo*, which means City of the Saint, because St. Anthony of Padua is buried in the basilica over there."

He pointed to a massive building across the piazza. It was a hodge-podge of styles—Gothic and Romanesque, mainly, with a definite Eastern flair that was heightened by the cupolas that adorned its roofs. A large statue of a man on a horse stood in front of the building.

"Is that St. Anthony?"

"No, it's Gattamelata. And before you ask, I have no idea who he is. That statue is famous because of the sculptor, Donatello. You're supposed to notice how realistic the horse is."

Samantha peered up at a huge stone horse, unable to avoid seeing what he was so obliquely referring to even in the gathering dusk. "Well, I'm no expert," she said, after a moment. "But I'd say that horse is a bit more, ah, realistic than any real one I've ever seen."

"That's because it's an Italian horse," Nick said, deadpan. "All Italians are more ah—" he mimicked her tone "—realistic in that area." He squeezed her shoulders again, stopping whatever laughing retort was on her lips. "Come on, let's go eat. I know you must be—"

"Starving," they both said at the same time.

They walked across the piazza and under another archway into the open-air grill area of the Ristorante Al Santo. They were promptly led inside to a small table set for two.

"Bring us a bottle of Cerasuolo del Piave," Nick said, naming a popular local rosé.

The waiter tucked the wine list back under his arm without missing a beat. "Would you like the menu now, *signor*, or later?"

"Now, *per piacere*." Nick handed a menu across the table to Samantha. "What do you think you'd like to eat?"

"Oh, I don't know. It all looks so good." She glanced down at the menu and then looked around at what was on the other diners' plates. "What's that?" She nodded in the direction of the next table.

Nick glanced over his shoulder. *"Bisato in tecia."*

Samantha raised her eyebrows.

"Eels cooked in tomatoes and herbs."

"Eels? You mean those slippery, snakey things?"

"Would you like to try it?" he said solicitously. "I know how you like to experience the authentic cuisine of a country."

"Uh, no thanks." Samantha hid behind her menu. "Not this time."

"Well, how about veal? Do you like that?"

Samantha put her menu down. It was written in Italian and she couldn't read it, anyway. "I'd love veal."

The waiter came back with their wine. Expertly he drew the cork out of the bottle and poured it into their glasses. Then he took their order with a soft, "Very good, *signor*," and slipped away with a lingering look at Samantha.

"He looks as if he'd like to carry you off," Nick remarked when the waiter was out of earshot. "Not that I blame him." He leaned across the tiny table, reaching out to tuck a strand of hair behind her ear. "Have I told you how lovely you look tonight?"

Her hands went to her hair. It felt as if it were sticking out in every direction. "A lovely mess," she said, making a little moue. "Maybe I should find a ladies' room and freshen up."

"No, leave it." His fingers curled around her arm, lowering it back to the table. "I like your hair all tousled. It makes you look like you just got out of bed." He paused, waiting until he had her full attention. "With me," he finished softly.

Samantha blushed, glancing around to see if anyone had overheard him. There were several men staring openly at her—simple admiration on the faces of some, blatant invitation on others. She looked away, down to where Nick's hand rested on her arm.

His fingers moved up and down the delicate ivory skin. "That's what every man in here thinks, you know. That we just got out of bed. They're all envying me my good fortune and wishing they were sitting here in my place." He felt a spurt of jealousy as the words formed on his lips. Hot, stinging jealousy that made him want to bundle her up and hide her away from all the admiring male stares.

So it's starting already, he thought. He had only just admitted his feelings to himself—the possibility of his feelings—and, already, he was losing control, thinking irrationally. Behaving like a man in love. A fool.

"Nick?" Samantha said, alarmed by the look on his face. "Nick, what is it?"

He shook his head. "Nothing." He withdrew his hand from her arm and nudged her wineglass toward her. "You haven't tasted your wine."

She picked up the glass by the stem. "To us," she said deliberately, holding his eyes as she waited for him to pick up his own glass.

It took a moment. A long moment. But Samantha's eyes never wavered. Never faltered. *There is an "us"*, she told herself fiercely. *There is!* And he would have to admit it sooner or later. He couldn't go on forever, pretending to himself that they were just having an affair.

Nick sighed softly and raised the glass to his lips. "To us," he said at last, wondering exactly what he meant by the words—and if she would hold him to them when their affair was over.

9

COVERED FROM NECK to toes in a gauzy white caftan, Samantha reclined on a cushioned chaise longue, thumbing idly through an Italian *Vogue* while she watched Nick's long, golden body cut through the sparkling blue water of the pool. The same nocturnal activities that had left her feeling deliciously languid and lazy had apparently invigorated him. He'd done half a dozen laps so far and showed no sign of slowing down.

A quick flip-turn jackknifed his narrow hips out of the water for a second as he began another lap, exposing the most miniscule pair of black racing briefs that she'd ever seen outside a magazine swimwear layout. They looked magnificent on him—or he looked magnificent in them, she thought, depending on how you looked at it.

She'd been a bit embarrassed when he first appeared in them, afraid that Marina or *Zia* Aida would catch her looking where she shouldn't. The feeling didn't last long, though, mostly because Nick himself seemed so totally unaware of the stunning picture he made and because his two female relatives never even batted an eye. Which wasn't surprising, since Marina's bathing suit was just as brief as her brother's.

Three tiny triangles of orange Lycra and a light golden tan were all that covered her thin body as she lay floating on a bright yellow rubber mat. One heel rested on the pool rim to anchor her to its edge. Her eyes were closed.

Samantha yawned lazily, her gaze wandering back over to where Nick was still doing laps. Water gilded the muscles of his arms and shoulders as they rippled under his skin. Sunlight glittered on his body, creating a sparkling halo of diamonds in the spray kicked up by his feet. Samantha closed her eyes, seeing him in her mind as he'd been last night, his muscles bulging with the effort of holding back, his sweat-sheened body gleaming in the candlelight that flickered from the nightstand.

"Makes you tired just to look at him, doesn't it?" Marina commented.

Samantha opened her eyes. "Exhausted," she agreed, turning to smile at the younger woman from under the brim of the wide straw hat that shaded her face.

"Still—" Marina levered herself up on the rubber mat and leaned back on her elbows "—it's nice to see someone really use the pool for a change." Her smile was inviting but somehow tentative as if, now that she'd started a conversation she didn't quite know how to keep it going.

Samantha quickly filled the silence. "Don't you use the pool very often?"

Marina shook her head. "Only for lounging by or floating on."

"Ah." Samantha smiled. "We're kindred spirits then."

Marina nodded.

Samantha cast around in her mind for something else to keep the conversation going. "Nick said you were his youngest sister when he introduced us yesterday. How many more are there?"

"Just one. Angie. Well, Angelina, really. She works at Gavino Industries in Research and Development."

"Maybe I met her. I met a lot of people at Gavino Industries."

Marina shook her head again. "I doubt it. Angie's been kind of antisocial since her second divorce."

"Oh. I see." Samantha decided that that was enough of that line of conversation. "And what do you do, Marina? When you're not lounging around the pool at an Italian villa, that is?"

"I was an art student before—" Marina's voice shook and her eyes took on that fragile, haunted look "—before I . . ."

Samantha sat up, swinging her feet over the side of the chaise. "Marina, I'm sorry. I didn't mean to pry." She leaned forward, concern clouding her eyes. "Forget I asked, okay? Let's talk about something else."

"No. No, it's all right. I have to learn to live with it, Nick says." With a quick contortion, she hoisted herself onto the tiled rim of the pool and pulled the mat up beside her. She continued speaking with her back to Samantha, her brown legs dangling into the water. "I was going to art school in New York. I wanted to be an illustrator in the advertising department at Gavino Industries. And then I met this guy. He was—" her shoulders hunched pathetically "—I fell in love with him."

Samantha shifted from the chaise, moving to crouch down beside the unhappy young woman. "Marina." Her hands hovered over the thin shoulders, afraid to touch her, afraid not to.

"I thought he fell in love with me, too. He acted like he had. I moved into his loft in Soho with him. It was kind of run-down and a little tacky but I fixed it up really nice with some of the income from my trust fund. Eric—that was his name, Eric—didn't have a regular job. He's an artist." She rubbed at her forehead. "Anyway, one day I came home from school early and found him in bed with the girl who lived downstairs." She looked up as Samantha's hands settled comfortingly on her shoulders. "I tried to kill myself."

"Oh, Marina."

"I guess Nick went sort of crazy when he found out." She looked back at the sparkling water. "He's always been the one who looked after all of us," she explained softly. "Our father died when I was a little girl and Nick sort of had to take over the family, you know?"

"I know," Samantha murmured, remembering that grainy newspaper photo sitting on top of her dresser in New York. His father had committed suicide over a love gone wrong; his youngest sister had tried the same thing. His mother and other sister had been divorced more than once. A great deal became very clear to her. "I know."

"I took pills. Eric didn't believe me. He thought I was bluffing, that I hadn't really taken anything. When I passed out he got scared and called the paramedics. I don't know how Nick found out, but he was at the hospital when they finished pumping my stomach. The doctors had to pull him off Eric." She looked up at Samantha, her brown eyes shimmering with unshed tears. "I haven't seen Eric since," she said softly.

"Oh, Marina." Samantha's arms went around her thin shoulders. "I'm sorry. So sorry," she soothed, not knowing what else to say. What could you say to a young woman who'd been through what she had?

Marina accepted the embrace for only a few moments. "It's okay." She straightened away from Samantha. "I'm okay." She sniffed and wiped at her eyes. "I *will* be okay," she said firmly. "I've been getting counseling and it's helped some." She glanced over to where her brother was hoisting himself out of the pool. Samantha's eyes followed the path Marina's had taken. "Nick has helped the most. Just knowing he's there for me, that he still loves me in spite of the mess I've made of everything, is what finally made me want to go on living."

He turned as if feeling their eyes on him, a smile on his lips. It faded as he read the expressions on their faces. It didn't take a genius to see that Samantha was offering comfort, nor to realize that Marina was on the verge of tears. He picked up a towel, rubbing at his wet hair as he walked around the pool to them.

"What are you two beauties plotting?" His smile was back in place but Samantha saw the concern in his eyes.

"Don't tell him," Marina whispered. "He'll only get upset." She splashed into the pool, striking out for the shallow end.

Samantha rose to her feet. "Nothing much," she said in answer to his question. "Marina was just giving me some tips on handling Italian men." She watched Marina as she climbed up the steps on the shallow end of the pool and hurried over the lawn to the house. Then she turned around and smiled at Nick. "One Italian man in particular."

"As if you needed any." He forced his eyes away from the retreating figure of his sister and lowered himself, face down, onto the chaise that Samantha had vacated. "Come spread some suntan lotion on my back."

"Certainly, O master of mine." She placed her palms together at her waist, bowing as she moved toward him.

He grinned in spite of himself. "Now that's exactly how to treat an Italian man," he said, and then sobered almost immediately. "But don't try to tell me that Marina told you that."

"I wouldn't even presume to try." Samantha sat down on the edge of the chaise, nudging him over a little with her hip, and began spreading the suntan lotion over the broad, brown muscles of his back. "I don't know why you bother with this stuff. You certainly don't need it."

"I like having you rub it in." He was quiet for a long moment, his cheek on the back of his hand, staring at the water as Samantha smoothed the lotion on his skin in slow, soothing circles.

"There." She swatted his bikini-clad rear. "All basted."

Nick turned over and caught her by the upper arms. The frustrated helplessness of a strong-willed man faced with a problem he couldn't solve with strength or will alone, filled his eyes. "Is she all right, Samantha? Is there anything bothering her that I don't know about? Anything new?"

Samantha touched his face with gentle fingers. "I'm no psychiatrist but I'd say she's as all right as she can be under the circumstances."

"She was crying."

Samantha nodded. "A little. But she's entitled to her tears, wouldn't you say? It hurts when love goes wrong."

His mouth twisted. "And it always goes wrong."

"No." Her fingers drifted between his brows, smoothing the line there. "Not always." She skimmed down his Roman nose to touch the curve of his upper lip, smiling when his mouth pursed in an unconscious kiss against her fingertips. "Not when you find the right person to love," she told him.

Their eyes held for a long, searching moment. "Is that a guarantee?" he asked softly. Longingly. He wanted to believe it was. With every fiber of his being, he wanted to believe that love between a man and a woman could result in something other than tragedy or farce.

Samantha leaned forward, bringing her face down to his, her head tilted so that the brim of her hat shaded them both. "An ironclad, no refunds, no excuses guaran-damn-tee," she said solemnly.

At that moment, he almost believed it. Dammit, he thought, lifting his head the few inches necessary to bring their lips together, he did believe it! Right now, anyway. When she looked at him, kissed him, he could believe anything.

"Nick! Samantha!" Aida hailed them from the terrace. "Your guests, they are here."

ROBBIE WAS STANDING a little apart from the group on the terrace, deliberately distancing himself from the rest of the party. He couldn't have announced his bad mood more loudly if he'd shouted it.

Oh, Lord, thought Samantha with a sigh, *here we go again.* She scrutinized him from under the brim of her hat as she crossed the lawn from the pool, trying to determine if he were having a run-of-the-mill bad mood or if it indicated something more serious. Then, no, she thought, giving her head a little shake, if he'd been shoplifting again he'd be flushed and excited, not sullen and withdrawn. Thank God for small favors.

"I'm glad to see that you all made it in one piece," Nick greeted his guests as he and Samantha mounted the terrace steps. "Or did you?" he added, noticing the makeup artist's pale cheeks and large dark sunglasses. "Lulu, you look a little, ah—" he smiled teasingly "—how do I put this tactfully?"

"There is no way to put it tactfully, luv," Lulu groaned. "I know I look like I've been dragged backwards through a hedgerow. It's all his fault, though." She pouted prettily at Jeffrey. "He swore that anisette—" she named a traditional French liqueur "—was no more potent than a tall gin and tonic."

The hair stylist grinned. "I lied," he said, reaching out to shake Nick's offered hand.

"Taylor." Nick acknowledged the male model with another handshake. "And Terri." He leaned down and kissed the production manager on the cheek.

Robbie was standing too far away to shake hands without Nick making a production of it. For a moment he considered doing just that, and then, in the very next

moment, decided against it; a confrontation would
only upset everyone for no good purpose. Besides, he
was feeling too relaxed and happy right now to let a
bad-tempered boy ruffle his feathers. He nodded at
Robbie, including the younger man in his general
greeting. "Welcome to the Villa Rosa, everyone."

"*Si, si. Benvenuto.*" *Zia* Aida added an enthusiastic
welcome. "Come. Sit." She waved them toward the
umbrella-shaded tables. "You must all be hungry after
such a long journey. We will eat *il pranzo*—lunch?—
very soon. In minutes only." She looked up at her
nephew. "If that is okay?"

Nick gave her a quick one-armed hug that had her
blushing. "That will be very okay." He smiled at the
assembled group. "And after lunch you can all change
into your bathing suits, or whatever, and we'll spend
the rest of the day lazing by the pool. How does that
sound? One more day of sloth before we get back to
work?"

Lulu sighed with exaggerated pleasure. "It sounds
absolutely heavenly."

"Lead me to the food," Terri said.

Everyone—almost everyone—moved toward the
tables.

"Robbie?" Samantha said, halting when she realized
he wasn't heading in the same direction as the rest of
them. She turned, following him to the low stone wall
that edged the terrace.

"Been having a good time?" he asked sullenly, staring out over the rose garden and the pool beyond.

"Yes, I have." She answered his question with as
much good humor as she could. "A very good time."

She leaned a hip against the wall. "Have you?" she asked, crossing her arms over her middle.

"Yeah, sure." He plucked a rose off the climbing vines and pulled off a petal, throwing it to the lawn. "It's been a real ball."

Samantha bit her tongue and counted to ten. "Where did you all go?" she said when it was obvious he wasn't going to offer the information.

He shrugged. "We went to a jazz club called the The Cool Blue, someplace that Jeff knew about," he said, plucking off another petal. It went sailing over the wall and onto the lawn. "And then Lulu wanted to go dancing—" another rose petal joined its fellows "—but that got pretty boring, so I took off on my own." He looked at her out of the corner of his eye as he made the last statement.

"Oh?" she said carefully. She knew what that look meant. He was daring her to ask if he'd broken his promise. She shifted her hip against the wall, fighting the urge to do just that. "Where'd you go?" she asked instead. That was surely general enough not to sound accusing.

He shrugged again, still watching her out of the corner of his eye. "Nowhere in particular." He leaned over the wall and opened his fingers. The rose, minus most of its petals, dropped to the lawn.

Samantha frowned at the fallen flower. "You must have gone somewhere," she said, trying not to sound suspicious, knowing full well that she did. But Robbie, damn him, was doing his level best to arouse her suspicions.

"Just around," he said evasively, reaching for another blossom.

Samantha's hand covered his, stopping him from further destruction of Aida's roses. "Just around?" she said skeptically.

He gave her an offended look. "I wasn't out shoplifting, if that's what you mean."

"I didn't say that."

"But you thought it," he accused.

Samantha sighed. Yes, she'd thought it. She couldn't deny that. And she was sorry she'd thought it, but in all fairness, she couldn't help but think it, given the way he was acting. She considered pointing that out to him and then changed her mind. He would only deny it.

She squeezed his hand lightly instead, half in apology, half in entreaty. "Let's go eat lunch, shall we?" she said. "*Zia* Aida is a wonderful cook."

"*Si*, come," Aida called, motioning them toward the tables when she saw them move away from the wall. "Come and eat."

"Everything all right?" Nick asked softly, turning toward Samantha as she settled into the chair next to his.

Samantha sighed. "Just fine," she said, looking down as she spread her napkin out on her lap.

"You're sure?" He bent closer, his hand reaching out to cover hers. "You don't sound just fine."

She looked up, warmed by his concern. "No, really, everything's fine." She turned her hand, lacing her fingers with his on her lap. "Robbie's just..." She shrugged, her voice trailing off as she tried and failed to come up with what Robbie just was.

"Robbie's just in love with you," Nick finished for her.

"No, he—"

Nick squeezed her hand. "Trust me on this, Samantha. The boy's in love with you and it's making him as miserable as a bear with a hangover."

"Oh, no, you're wrong, Ni—"

He smiled suddenly, warmly, leaving her open-mouthed in mid-word. "Not that I blame him, mind you. It's hard not to be."

"Nick!" she said softly, stunned and beguiled by his near admission. It was the closest he'd ever come to admitting his feelings for her. She lifted her free hand and touched his cheek. "Oh, Nick, I—"

"I don't think I can eat anymore," Robbie said loudly.

Almost as one, Nick and Samantha turned to look at him. Their fingers were still entwined on her lap, her hand was still touching his cheek, their eyes were still full of the wonder of each other.

Robbie's light hazel eyes were narrowed and fierce. "I think I'm getting a sick headache."

"Sick?" Samantha echoed uncertainly. He didn't look sick to her. He looked as if he were about to explode.

Aida glanced at her nephew. "Headache?" she said.

"*Il mal di testa,*" Nick translated.

"Ah, poor boy." Aida was all bustling concern. "It is this hot sun," she said, getting up from her place at the table to come around to him. "Come, you must lie down in the coolness of the house, *si*? And I will bring you a cold cloth for your head. And then some *brodo*, ah—" she looked at her nephew again, "—broth?"

Nick nodded.

"Some nice broth," she said as she put a motherly arm around Robbie, "to eat when you are feeling better."

Samantha watched them go, a sad, sick, twisted feeling building in her stomach. *Why, Nick just might be right*, she thought, incredulous.

Robbie's last look before Aida led him away had been one of pure, fierce, undiluted jealousy—the kind a man only feels when he's locked in a bitter struggle with another man over the same woman.

SEVERAL HOURS LATER Samantha tapped softly on the bedroom door. She had stopped by earlier, twice, but both times there'd been silence behind the door and she'd gone away, afraid—hopeful—that he'd really been resting. Now, however, the muffled sound of heavy rock music announced the fact that he was definitely awake.

"Robbie, can I come in?"

There was no answer.

She tapped again, louder. "Robbie, please let me come in. I want to talk to you."

"Go away. I don't want to talk to you." His voice was a hoarse, angry whisper but she heard him quite clearly over the muted blare of the discordant music.

"Robbie," she persisted. "Please let me in. We've got to talk."

"Leave me alone."

Samantha was sorely tempted to do just that except that it wouldn't have solved anything. Robbie and his problems weren't about to go away; they would only get worse if someone—if she—didn't do something about them. She had to tell him this . . . this *feeling* he had for her would never, ever be reciprocated.

"I'll stand here all day if I have to." She hit the door with the flat of her hand. "Now let me in."

"All right. All right." The door opened a crack. "Okay, so talk."

"I'm not going to talk standing in the hall. Let me in."

He yanked the door open, giving her a mocking bow. "The Sophisticated Lady's wish is my command."

The room was dim, lit only by what late-afternoon sunlight managed to penetrate the closed brocade drapes. The rock music was loud and heavy on the base. She stepped into the room, blinking as her eyes adjusted to the lack of light. Robbie slammed the door behind her.

She turned to him, opening her mouth to reprimand him for his rudeness to Nick and his family, for the rumpled condition of the beautiful cream and pale green guest room, for the loud music, for slamming the door. His face stopped her. His eyes were bleary and red rimmed.

Her hand went out to him in quick concern. "Robbie, are you all right?"

He shook her off. "What do you care?" He turned toward the rumpled bed and threw himself onto it, staring up at the ceiling as if he were alone, like a little boy who was trying to punish his mother by ignoring her.

Samantha sat down on the edge of the bed and leaned over to switch off the cassette player. "I *do* care, Robbie. You know that," she said, unconsciously speaking to him as if he were no more than a tired, sulking child.

She reached out, smoothing back the hair on his forehead as she'd done so many times before.

He knocked her hand away. "Lay off," he said, throwing his arm across his eyes.

"All right, Robbie. I'm sorry. I won't touch you." She folded her hands on her lap and wondered what to do next. He looked so defeated that her tender heart ached for him. There was no denying he loved her—or thought he did—she realized that quite clearly now. And not as a brother, as she had always thought, but as a man. Also, quite clearly, he was suffering because of that love.

But that didn't excuse his behavior, did it? No, definitely not. Other people handled unrequited love without becoming insufferably rude, or shoplifting or— She thought suddenly of Marina and fear clutched at her heart. Robbie wouldn't resort to that, would he?

She looked at him, lying there on the rumpled bed with his arm over his eyes. No, Robbie wouldn't resort to self-destruction. He would rant and rave, sulk and brood and generally make things miserable for everybody, but he wouldn't do anything quite so final.

So, how do I handle him?

"Robbie, I'm sorry." Her voice was softer than usual. Her hands were clasped tightly in her lap. It was better not to touch him at all, she thought, since she couldn't touch him in the way he so obviously wanted her to. "I don't know what else to say except that I'm sorry."

He didn't move, didn't give any indication that he'd heard her.

"I didn't ask to—" she hesitated. Would she hurt him more by saying it? Maybe she would, but it had to be said. Had to be out in the open. "I didn't ask to fall in love with Nick. It just happened."

"So, it's love, is it?" His voice was harsh and mocking and thick with innuendo.

"Yes." Samantha's voice was soft but firm. "I love him."

"And I suppose he loves you, right?" He removed his arm from across his eyes to look up at her.

Samantha hesitated. He loved her, yes, but he hadn't said it yet.

"Has he said he loves you?" Robbie demanded when she didn't answer.

"No, he hasn't." She glanced at him and looked quickly away again. She didn't like the look in his eyes. "He does, though."

"Don't make me laugh." Robbie sat up suddenly, his fingers digging into her cheeks as he turned her face to his. "He isn't going to tell you he loves you," he said cruelly, "because he doesn't. Gavino's the kind who has dozens of women just like you. Dozens!" he taunted her. "You're nothing to him but a toy. You know that, don't you, Sophisticated Lady?" His tone made a curse of the name. "A sexy playmate to pass the time until he goes back to New York. And when he does you'll be yesterday's news. Another notch on the old bedpost."

Samantha jerked her chin out of his hand. "That's not true! Nick isn't like that."

Robbie grabbed her wrist to keep her from rising. "Who're you trying to convince? Me or yourself?"

She tried to pull her wrist away. Tears shimmered in her eyes, threatening to spill over. "Let go of me, Robbie," she said quietly.

His fingers gentled on her wrist but he didn't let go. "Oh, Sammie. I'm sorry." He tried to draw her into his embrace but she resisted him. "I'm sorry. Don't cry. He's not worth it, Sammie. Don't cry."

"I'm not crying for him, you idiot," she said, her arms stiff as she held herself from his embrace. "I'm crying for us. For you. For what we've just lost."

"Don't say that!" he cried passionately. "We haven't lost anything." He cupped her face in his hands. "I love you, Samantha."

She kept her eyes stubbornly lowered. "I'm sorry, Robbie," was all she could say.

"Damn him!" Robbie's hands clasped hers tightly. Too tightly. "Damn him! If it wasn't for Gavino you'd be my—"

"No, Robbie." She looked into his face then. "Even if I'd never met Nick there would still be no 'us.' Can't you understand that?"

"But I love you," he said, as if he expected that to change everything.

"And I love you. As my brother."

"But—"

"As my brother, Robbie," she said, looking into his eyes with a sad, serious expression. She slipped her hands out from under his and stood up. "I'm sorry." She turned to go.

"Wait a minute." He jumped up from the bed. "You might as well take this with you." He dug his hand into the pocket of his baggy parachute pants and threw something on the bed. A gold Cross pen, a mono-grammed money clip and a pair of antique gold cuff links with roses engraved on them tumbled across the bedspread.

Samantha's eyes widened. The Cross pen was Terri's. The money clip bore the initials JCW; it had to belong to Jeffrey. And the last time she'd seen the cuff links they'd been lying in a small, ebony tray on the dresser in Nick's bedroom. She looked up at Robbie, her eyes full of stunned disbelief. "When did you—"

"There's more," Robbie said, interrupting her. He hauled a camera bag onto the bed and snapped it open. "This." A zoom lens for a make of camera he didn't even own bounced on the bed. "And these." Three silk ties with designer labels. "And this." A crystal paperweight.

"Robbie." She sank down on the edge of the bed, reaching out to touch each item as if she couldn't believe what she was seeing. "Oh, Robbie." She looked up at him.

He stared back with a sort of frenzied bravado, daring her to . . . to what? she wondered.

"I'm going to have to tell Nick about this," she said. "He'll have to know about this now."

"You can't." Robbie pointed at the camera lens. It was large and ungainly and, she knew, hideously expensive. "That makes it grand larceny. You wouldn't want me thrown in an Italian jail, would you?"

Her eyes hardened at his blatant attempt at manipulation. "I don't know. Maybe that would be the best place for you."

Robbie stared at her as if trying to judge how serious she was. "You don't mean that," he said, but he didn't sound altogether sure.

Samantha saw her advantage and pressed it. Maybe she could scare him into going straight, at least for the time they had left in Europe. When they got home she'd see that he got professional help. "Are you willing to bet on that?"

"You wouldn't."

She stood up. "You lose," she said, heading for the door.

Robbie grabbed the sleeve of her gauzy caftan. "Sammie, wait."

"Wait for what?" She stared at him, steely-eyed.

"Sammie, you're my friend. My sister." He released the fabric of her caftan to curl his fingers around her arm. "You can't turn me in. The least Gavino'll do is fire me on the spot. If he doesn't turn me in to the Italian cops first. And I can't lose this job, Sammie. I can't." His fingers bit into her wrist. His eyes were wide with cunning and entreaty and the beginnings of real fear.

She stared back at him, dismayed and undecided. What to do? What to say? How to handle this whole sorry mess?

"Sammie, please." Incredibly, he began to cry. He let go of her wrist and dropped to the bed, leaning his elbows on his knees. A soft, whimpering sound came from behind his concealing hands. It tore at Samantha's heart.

No matter what he'd done, he was her brother. Part of her family. And she loved him. Somehow, she had to handle this. But how? Should she go to Nick and risk having him fire Robbie on the spot? Should she keep it to herself and hope she could smooth things over until they got back to New York and she could make sure

Robbie got professional help? They only had one more week in Europe and then they'd be headed home. One more week. Surely she could handle it for that long. Surely just one more week wouldn't matter if it meant saving Robbie's career?

"It's all your fault, anyway." Robbie's voice held a whining note now, accusing her. "It's all your fault."

"My fault?"

"I did it because of you. This time it was because of you. I couldn't stand the thought of Gavino and you together...in bed together." He looked up, his eyes wild and teary. "It's all your fault."

Oh, God! *Was* it her fault? Even a little? Common sense told her no. She wasn't responsible for Robbie's feelings. His problem stemmed from insecurity and weakness and it had started long before they'd become stepbrother and sister, long before he'd begun to think he was in love with her, long before either of them had ever heard of Nick Gavino. But when he looked at her like that, with pain and fear and accusation in his eyes, common sense had very little chance.

She *felt* as if it was her fault. Maybe she could have prevented it. Somehow. If she'd been less wrapped up in Nick, less concerned with her own feelings, she might have seen what was happening sooner and been able to do something.

"Sammie?" He sounded so tired, and his face, turned up to hers, was hopeful. "Are you going to turn me in to Gavino?"

Samantha sighed, knowing she was going to cover for him one more time. "No," she said wearily. "But this is the last time, Robbie. I won't cover for you again."

He wiped at his nose with the back of his hand. "You won't have to cover for me again, Sammie. This is the last time. I promise."

"You promised before," she reminded him.

"But this time I really mean it," he vowed. "This time I . . ." He faltered and looked down at the floor between his feet, unable to meet her steady gaze. "I won't do anything else to upset you, Sammie," he said quietly. "I promise."

"We'll see," she murmured, leaning over to scoop the small gold items off the bed.

She returned to her own room a few minutes later, the small cache of stolen goods in her hands. She couldn't do anything about the things he'd stolen from the stores, and she wasn't going to try, but she could return the personal items he'd taken from the other members of the crew. Somehow.

Nick's cuff links were easy. She could just put them back on the ebony trinket tray in his bedroom and hope he never realized they'd even been missing. The other items were harder. She stood indecisively in the middle of her room, trying to decide what to do with them until she could return them to their rightful owners. A knock sounded on her door.

"Samantha?" Nick's deep voice came through the door.

"Just a minute," she called, surprising herself with the steadiness of her voice.

Hide them! Her eyes darted around the room. She had to hide them! Her purse lay on top of the dressing table. Hurriedly she stuffed the small gold items inside it, then dropped the leather shoulder bag on the floor and kicked it under the dressing table for good measure. Swiftly, she crossed to the bed and yanked down the spread, punching the pillow to make it look as if she'd been lying down.

"Nick." She opened the door, smiling a little shakily into his face. "I'm sorry to make you wait so long. I was lying down," she lied, hating herself. "And I...I wanted to run a brush through my hair."

He touched her hair, smoothing it under his palm. "You know I like it best when it's all messed up." He bent his head and kissed her lightly on the mouth. "But it looks beautiful any way you wear it." His hand skimmed down the back of her head to her nape, tilting her head up. He kissed her again, a little more thoroughly this time, and then drew back to look into her face. "What's the matter, Samantha?"

"Nothing," she said, looking down at the dark triangle of hair exposed by the modest V-neck of his sports shirt. She fingered his top button.

He covered her hand with his, stilling it. "You seem a little preoccupied." His lips touched her forehead and then her nose, tenderly and without passion. "Was Robbie very difficult?"

Oh, Nick, if you only knew how difficult!

She leaned into him, hiding her face in the curve of his strong, brown throat. "It's all right now," she said, nuzzling into him. And, strangely, it was. Almost. "We talked it out and I think we understand each other now." *I hope we do.* "I told him that there can never be anything more between us than there already is. He didn't like it but at least he knows now that I'll never love him as anything but a brother."

"That's good." Nick kneaded her back, his hands sliding over the caftan in a soothing motion. His lips touched her ear. "I came in here to invite you to dinner," he said. "I thought we'd try another one of Padua's restaurants. You and me and Marina and *Zia* Aida and the whole crew. Make it a real party. How does that sound?"

"That sounds lovely." She wrapped her arms around his lean waist. He was such a caring, sensitive man, whether he knew it or not, and she felt like such a conniving, deceiving sneak.

I'll tell him about Robbie, she decided suddenly. *When we get back to New York, I'll tell him. He'll understand. I hope.*

"Even Robbie's invited," he said into her hair.

"I don't think Robbie will want to come."

Nick drew back to smile at her. "I can't say I'm sorry about that."

"Neither am I," she said.

10

THEY ATE DINNER at a charming little trattoria in the hills just outside of Padua, sitting in the dappled shade of a grape arbor in what was, essentially, the terraced backyard of the family who owned the small restaurant. There was an excellent, if short, wine list but no menus as the meal served was set and depended on whatever had been freshest at the market that morning.

Tonight, the hostess explained in halting English as two young girls placed the first platters on the table, they would feast on antipasto of thin slices of tightly rolled mortadella and prosciutto, a judicious selection of cheeses, homemade breadsticks, roasted peppers, olives, marinated mushrooms and garlic-spiced strips of grilled zucchini. Later, she promised, there would be a creamy risotto flavored with Parmesan cheese, a green salad with tomatoes from her own garden, and fresh-caught *orata*, cooked with mussels and crayfish and seasoned with just a touch of curry. And, for dessert— she touched her fingers to her pursed lips, then flared them outward, her eyes closed in pretended bliss—two flavors of homemade *gelati*, Italy's version of ice cream.

It all sounded wonderful but, for one of the few times in her life, Samantha couldn't summon up any interest in food. Authentic cuisine or otherwise.

Robbie had decided to come to dinner with them.

If that had surprised her—and it had—she was even more surprised by his seeming amiability during the evening. She tried to be glad for small favors, telling herself that his air of determined goodwill meant that he was making a sincere effort to be pleasant.

He was on his best behavior, there was no doubt about that. He chatted easily to Marina and Terri, who sat on either side of him at the long trestle-style table; he joined in the laughter at Lulu's droll jokes; he was even civil to Nick, who sat at the table's head. Barely civil, true, but at least he appeared to be trying, she thought, pushing a piece of fish around on her plate with the tines of her fork as she tried not to watch him too obviously.

If it wasn't for the somehow furtive gleam in his eyes when she caught his glance across the table, Samantha might have accepted his change of heart at face value. But there was just too much difference between this Robbie and the one she'd left, despondent and angry, in his bedroom.

And yet . . . He *had* promised not to do anything else to upset her, hadn't he? Never mind that he'd already broken one promise to her, she thought, pushing the memory of that incident away. This time he'd shown real remorse. This time he'd really meant it. She hoped.

She glanced across the table again, catching him with his head bent attentively toward Marina, who was talking quietly, one hand gesturing outward as she spoke. Robbie looked up just then, his eyes searching out Samantha's. He smiled when he caught her looking at him. It was a quick, satisfied smile, an almost sly smile, and then, quite deliberately, he turned his attention back to Marina.

She wished she knew what he was up to!

"I'm glad Robbie's finally realized that you're not available," Nick whispered in her ear as she sat there, fingering the stem of her wineglass as she frowned at her stepbrother's bent head, "but I'd prefer that his eye had landed on someone other than Marina."

Samantha jerked her head around and stared at Nick. Of course! That was it! She couldn't believe she hadn't figured it out for herself. Robbie was using Marina— trying to use Marina—to get back at *her*. That's what that furtively defiant gleam in his eyes was all about, that almost sly, I'll-show-you-I-don't-care smile.

Oh, Robbie, she thought, torn between amusement and annoyance at his adolescent tactics, *as if that would make any difference at all.*

"Marina's too vulnerable right now to get involved in another relationship," Nick said, his brow furrowing as he watched his sister and her attentive seatmate. "Especially when he's only using her to make you jealous."

"It's all right." She lifted her wineglass and took a sip, appreciating the excellent Chianti Classico for the first time that evening. "It isn't working," she said to Nick.

"Not where you're concerned," he agreed, his eyes still focused halfway down the table. "But Marina's a different story. And the last thing she needs is another temperamental artistic type messing up her mind." His frown deepened as Marina reached out and patted Robbie's hand where it lay on the table. "Maybe I should get her to move down here."

"Take it easy, big brother," Samantha advised, picking up her fork. Her appetite seemed to have been completely restored by knowing exactly what Robbie was up to. "It isn't working with Marina, either," she told him, her eyes on her plate as she decided what to try first.

"What?" He turned his head toward her. Immediately, his expression softened. She was so beautiful, sitting there in the filtered light, with her lashes making lacy shadows on her cheeks and her lips wet with wine. It made him feel good just to look at her, despite his concern about Marina and even though he knew full well that to feel that way was only asking for trouble. "What isn't working with Marina?"

"Robbie's little Romeo routine. She isn't buying it." She lifted a forkful of the risotto to her lips. Rich, smooth cream and the sharp taste of Parmesan cheese soothed her neglected taste buds. She sighed.

Nick glanced back down the table. "How can you tell she isn't buying it? They look pretty chummy to me."

Samantha had to swallow before she could answer him. "Maybe," she agreed. "But she isn't flirting with him, she's just being—" she tilted her head consideringly "—polite. If I had to guess," she added after another mouthful of risotto, "I'd say they were probably discussing something like books they've read or movies they—" She laughed softly as she caught the quick, veiled look that Marina shot across the table. "Poor Robbie," she murmured.

"Why 'poor Robbie'?" Nick demanded.

"Because he seems to be striking out on all counts. Not only is Marina not flirting with him, she's doing her best to flirt with Jeffrey."

"What?" he said, louder than he had intended.

Aida and the restaurant hostess, who had pulled up a chair so that they could more easily discuss cooking, looked up inquiringly, as if to ask what he wanted.

He shook his head at them and hitched his chair closer to Samantha's. "What makes you say she's flirting with Jeffrey?" he asked almost irritably, annoyed with himself for being more disturbed by his feelings for Samantha than his concern over his sister.

"Well, not flirting, exactly," Samantha said soothingly. "But she's definitely interested." She leaned toward him conspiratorially, her hand reaching out to touch his forearm again. "Watch," she whispered.

Nick watched. But his hot-coffee eyes weren't directed at the other end of the table. They looked no farther than the hand on his arm. It was smooth and cool and pale against his rougher, darker skin, abruptly making him think of all the other exciting contrasts between their two bodies. Desire knifed through him and his brief irritation flared to anger for a moment—at himself, for his weakness in wanting her so fiercely— at her, for making him want with just a touch.

"There, see?" Samantha squeezed his arm, unaware of the emotions seething through him.

His anger fled just as abruptly as it had come, leaving behind only the feeling that had caused it.

"She's talking to Robbie but she's watching Jeffrey." Another low, soft laugh escaped Samantha. "And he's watching her." She reached for her wineglass with her

free hand, lifting it to her lips as she turned back toward Nick. "I'd say you're worrying about the wr—"
She broke off as their eyes met over a distance of inches.
"What?" she murmured, suddenly dry-mouthed, despite the warm, red wine she'd just swallowed. "What is it?"

"I want you," he said.

Samantha's eyes widened and her appetite deserted her for the second time that evening.

THREE HOURS LATER, Samantha sat at the dressing table in her room, a completely different kind of appetite tugging insistently at her insides as Nick stood behind her and slowly brushed her hair.

Dinner had seemed to last forever, and then there had been the long drive home and the bottomless cups of frothy cappuccino and bit-sized anise cookies out on the terrace that Aida had insisted were needed to make the evening complete.

But all Samantha had needed was Nick.

And, perversely, after the long looks and fleeting touches that had roused her to the tingling edge of excitement, he'd kept her waiting, too, insisting that they "prepare" separately, as if tonight were unique and special.

She had bathed first, filling the bathroom with a cloud of fragrant steam, and then retired, alone, to her bedroom, to perfume and primp. In a kind of sensual daze, she'd smoothed lotion into every inch of her long body, slipped into the black silk pajamas that she'd first worn in Paris and sat down at the dressing table to brush her hair while she waited for her lover to come to her.

And then he was there, reflected behind her in the mirror, his body wrapped in a white terrycloth robe, his hair still damp from his shower, his hand reaching out to take the hairbrush from hers. "Close your eyes," he said softly.

Obediently Samantha closed her eyes and let herself be soothed by the steady, rhythmic pull of the brush through her hair. A minute went by in silence, and then another. The brush slid easily through her hair, his following hand gliding along behind it. Samantha drifted deeper into the sensual fog that had begun to surround her when she'd looked into his hot eyes in the shade of the grape arbor.

"You have beautiful hair." Nick lifted the ends of her hair with the brush and let it drift back down. "Angel hair."

"Mm-mm," she murmured, silently urging him to go on with the brushing.

Nick twined a fistful of her hair in his hand and gently tugged on it, tilting her head backwards. "You have a beautiful face, too."

She smiled dreamily but didn't open her eyes.

He leaned over her, his body pressing against her shoulder as he put the brush on the dressing table. "A beautiful neck." One finger trailed down the line of her alabaster throat to the V of her pajama top. "A beautiful chest." His hand slipped under the loose black silk to close possessively over one breast. "Beautiful breasts." He stroked her nipple with his thumb. "Is there anything about you that isn't beautiful?"

Samantha sighed and opened one eye. "I have big feet." The words were teasing but her voice was thick with desire.

"Big feet? Really?" Nick withdrew his hand from inside her pajama top. Bending down, he slipped it under her knees and lifted her into his arms. "I hadn't noticed that."

Samantha looped her arms around his neck and laid her head on his shoulder. Her eyes closed again. "That's because you've never looked at my feet."

"I haven't?"

"No." She shook her head against his shoulder, breathing in the clean, male fragrance of him. "You've neglected my feet."

Nick laid her on the bed, dropping a kiss on her nose as he withdrew from her encircling arms. "Poor neglected little feet," he said.

"Big feet," she corrected lazily, stretching like a cat as Nick's hand skimmed down the silk-clad contours of her leg.

His fingers curled around her foot, the one farthest from him. He lifted it to his mouth, causing her knee to bend outward, and kissed the instep.

Samantha stilled in mid-stretch, her arms above her head.

"Poor neglected feet." His tongue traced a light path up the middle of her smooth, pink sole to the ball of her foot.

Her toes curled. It had never occurred to her before that the bottom of her foot was an erogenous zone but apparently it was. Incredibly so.

Nick's tongue flicked along the crease where her toes were attached to the rest of her foot. He placed tiny, deliberate kisses on the tip of each pedicured toe. He nibbled at the fine bones of her slender ankle and back down along the top of her foot until he reached her toes again. And then he sucked her big toe into his mouth.

Samantha felt the erotic pull of his mouth run all the way up her leg. Her foot jerked convulsively in his hand. Her fingers curled into the sheet beneath her.

"Nick," she gasped. "Nick, stop it. You're crazy." Another shudder passed through her as he continued his sensuous assault on her foot. "You're making me crazy."

He lifted his head, his hand still curled around her ankle. "You don't like it?"

"No. I mean yes, I like it but . . ."

"But you want something else, hmm? Something more?" He freed her ankle and began sliding his hand up under the silken pantleg of her pajama bottoms. "So do I."

She felt his fingers caress her smooth calf, felt them tickle lightly, maddeningly, against the back of her knee, and then his hand was stopped by the bunching material of her pajamas.

"What are you wearing these for?" he murmured. "Here, let me help you take them off."

In one smooth motion he withdrew his hand from her pantleg, hooked his fingers inside the elastic waistband of her pajama and pulled them slowly—oh so slowly—down her hips and legs and tingling, sensitized feet. He dropped the offending garment inside-out onto the floor.

"Much better." He ran his hands back up her bare legs, caressing her ivory thighs, just brushing the triangle of blond hair between them, sliding up until his fingers rested just below the hem of her pajama top.

"I still can't see all of you. I want to see all of you." He unbuttoned her pajama top from the bottom up as slowly as he'd removed the bottoms, finally spreading the two halves wide so that her small, creamy breasts were revealed to his avid gaze.

"So beautiful," he breathed. "Like something made of the rarest, finest porcelain." He trailed the tip of one finger over and around her breasts as he spoke, circling closer and closer to the budding pink nipples. They pebbled enticingly. "But so alive. So warm."

Samantha lay very still, barely breathing, looking into his face as he caressed her. His pupils were so enlarged that they almost obscured the warm brown irises of his eyes. She could see herself reflected there, aroused and arousing, her arms outflung like a willing sacrifice, her hair spread out on the pillows, her pale body framed by the black silk of her open pajama top.

She lifted her hand and tugged at the lapel of his robe. "Why are you wearing that thing?"

"Don't you like it?" His voice was deep and rasping, his eyes half-closed.

"No. Take it off," she ordered.

Nick shook his head. His seductive half smile, his heavy-lidded eyes, teased her, tempted her. "You take it off."

She reached up, grasping the end of the sash that held his robe together, pulling at it until the loose knot gave way. She looked up at his face, then, as if expecting him to do the rest.

Nick shook his head again. "You do it."

She sat up, her knees bent under her as she leaned forward to open the robe and push it off his shoulders. Her hands, palms flat against his skin, fingers spread, followed the fabric down the hard muscles of his arms to the bed. Then she sat back on her heels and looked at him, staring as if it had been days, instead of merely hours, since she had last seen him like this, his body bare and hard and hungry for hers. As naturally as breathing, she leaned forward and kissed him.

Nick reacted instantly, all thoughts of a leisured seduction forgotten as he surged forward to push her backward onto the bed.

"No." She put her hands on his chest. "Not yet."

Nick checked his forward movement and waited, breathless, for whatever she would do next. She had never taken the lead in their lovemaking before; he'd never let her take the lead. But tonight was different. Tonight was the start of a whole new phase in their relationship. Tonight was special because, tonight, he was finally ready to give up some of his formidable control and let someone else show him the way.

Slowly, as if sensing how important the moment was, she took one of his hands in both of hers and lifted it to her mouth. She kissed the back of it, brushing her lips across the knuckles, then turned it over and pressed her lips into his damp palm.

His fingers curled against her cheek. "Samantha." There was a wealth of meaning, of longing, of love in the way he said her name.

"I know," she breathed. "I know."

Amazed, he wondered if she'd known all along what he was just beginning to realize. Wondered, too, why it had taken him so long to see it. And then she touched her lips to the vein pulsing in his wrist, trailing soft, sweet kisses along the inside of his arm and he could wonder about nothing except what she might do to him next.

Her tongue flicked out, teasing the bend of his elbow. Even in a man as strong as Nick, she thought, that bit of skin seemed somehow tender and vulnerable. "Mm-mm," she said throatily. "You're delicious."

Her lips continued up his arm, pausing briefly to nibble at his powerful biceps. She raised herself higher on her knees, leaning forward slightly to trail her moist, open mouth over the top of his shoulder, stopping where it curved into his neck to feast on his salty sweetness.

He groaned, his body tightening like a bow string under her moist, caressing lips and the slender fingertips that rested on his shoulders.

She twined her arms loosely around his neck, brushing the tops of his shoulders with her inner arms, moving her body so that her hardened nipples rubbed lightly, back and forth across his chest. Her lips teased at his ear, her tongue delicately outlining its curves before thrusting inside.

Nick drew his breath in sharply. She was driving him crazy with her teasing touches. Deliciously, deliriously, seriously crazy. His skin itched. His ears buzzed. His heart hammered inside his chest. He slipped his hands inside her open pajama top, his fingers wrapping around her waist, and yanked her to him.

"No." Samantha stopped him with that one soft word. Her hands went to his shoulders, pushing, and Nick did as she directed, lying back against the sheets.

His dark eyes gleamed, hot and impatient and eager, as he looked up at her. They seemed to be devouring her face, feature by feature. "Now what?" His voice was a low, husky growl.

Samantha didn't answer him in words. Instead, she bent over his supine form, her mouth taking up where she'd left off. Her tongue ravished his ear with delicate precision. She nibbled at his hard jawline, pressed butterfly kisses over his eyes and nose and fresh-shaven cheeks, traced the strong line of his throat with her eager lips. She wanted to learn all of him, as he had learned her. Wanted to kiss all of him.

Her mouth moved down across his chest, teasing at the crisp, curling hairs until she found one of his flat, male nipples. Her tongue came out to taste it.

His hand moved to touch her, urging her down beside him.

"No," she said again. She pushed his hand away. "Lie still, darling." It was the first time she'd offered an endearment, knowing how it would have scared him off. But it wouldn't scare him now and, somehow, she knew it. "Lie still, darling," she repeated softly.

Her lips found his other nipple, sucking gently as it hardened in her mouth. Her hand, passive until now, began a slow exploration of his ribcage. It followed the mat of his thick chest hair until it narrowed on his flat belly. The tip of one finger dipped delicately into the

well of his navel. She felt his stomach muscles quiver
and he moaned softly. It was a sound that came from
deep inside him. She could feel his chest heaving under
her exploring lips as he struggled to control his breathing. His heart was thudding like a drum.

She was breathing heavily now, too, making little
panting sounds of pleasure and excitement. It thrilled
her immeasurably to know that she could bring him to
such a pitch of masculine arousal. She wanted to give
him more, much more. She wanted to love him in every
way there was.

Her hand moved lower and Nick seemed to stop
breathing for an endless minute. She touched him, her
fingers closing firmly around his turgid flesh. Nick began to tremble, his strong, virile body literally quak-
ing under the ministrations of her hand and lips. He
moaned again. And then yet again as Samantha's
mouth began to follow the path her hand had taken.

A long delirious moment later, he reached for her,
gripping her waist between his two hands, intending to
turn her onto her back. "Now, Samantha! I've got to
have you now! Right now! You're driving me crazy."

Samantha didn't make him wait any longer. It would
have been impossible because she couldn't wait any
longer, either. Resisting the pull of his hands, she raised
up to her knees and threw one slim leg across his hips.
His hands shifted to her hips as he realized her intent,
positioning her to receive him. A hiss of pleasure escaped her as she felt his hardness surge into her. A gut-
tural cry of ecstasy rose to his lips as her incredible
softness surrounded him.

"Samantha! Oh, God, Samantha!"

"Nick...Nick...Nick." His name became a rhythmic love chant as she lost herself in a swirling whirlpool of passionate, feminine need. Need that could only be assuaged by one man. This man. Her man.

"Nick!" Her voice rose to a crescendo—a high, wailing sound of pure pleasure. Vaguely she heard him answer her, felt his hands bite into her hips, felt his body tense as fulfillment arched her back and sent her spiraling through time and space. She hovered there for an endless moment, unconsciously straining for that last, elusive bit of satisfaction.

"Samantha, my love," Nick called out, his voice thick with emotion and soul-searing pleasure. "My sweet love."

She collapsed onto his sweaty, heaving chest, depleted and replete, weak and renewed, drained and exhilarated all at once. *Samantha, my love!* Were there any three sweeter words in the world?

"I love you," Nick said then, proving that there were. Almost frantically, he brushed her hair back with his palms, lifting her head in his hands so that he could look into her eyes. "I love you, Samantha. I love you." The emotion pouring out of him was frightening but he couldn't seem to stop saying the words. It was as if a dam had burst, washing away all of his hard-won control. "I love you."

"I know." She kissed his eyelids, one and then the other. His cheeks. His strong, Roman legionnaire's nose. His beautiful, vulnerable mouth. "I know, darling. I love you, too."

"Do you?" he asked, just to hear her say it again.

"I do." She nipped at his bottom lip. "I do," she said again, suddenly as giddily, helplessly euphoric as if there were a magnum of champagne bubbling through her veins. "I really, really—" she interspersed each really with a smacking kiss "—really do."

Happiness shone in his eyes, turning up his lips at the corners. "Show me."

Samantha giggled in pure, feminine delight. "I thought I just did," she said and giggled again.

"Feeling pleased with yourself, are you?" Nick wrapped his arms around her back and squeezed her with mock ferociousness. He was feeling pretty pleased with himself, too. He couldn't remember the last time he had felt so pleased with himself. With the world. "Think you've got me where you want me, do you?"

Samantha nodded smugly.

"We'll just see about that." He tightened his arms and rolled over, trapping her beneath him.

She clutched at his shoulders. "Nick?"

"Think I'm putty in your hands, do you?"

"Well, not exactly putty," she began.

He tickled her, his big hands running feather-light up and down her ribcage.

"No. Nick, no." Samantha fought him off weakly, nearly helpless with laughter. "No, don't. Nick!" She tried to grasp his hands.

"Let a woman get on top, just once, and she starts thinking you're a wimp," he growled playfully.

"Stop. I give up. I'll never get on top again." She hiccuped. "Nick, stop."

He became suddenly still. "Never again?" he said. His voice had an exaggerated, little boy mournful note. "Not even if I'm extra good?"

"Oh, you!" Samantha punched his shoulder, pushing him to one side, and wriggled out from under him. She sat up, cross-legged on the bed, and looked at him out of the corner of her eye.

Nick lay back, his hands under his head, watching her. "What?" he said.

"Well," Samantha tilted her head sideways. "You're not going to believe this but—" she shrugged, her hands held palms up "—I'm hungry."

Nick laughed delightedly. "Oh, I believe it all right. I'm surprised you went this long without adequate nourishment."

Samantha stuck her tongue out at him and got up from the bed.

"Where are you going? To raid the fridge?"

"Uh-uh. Need to find my purse." She glanced around the room, absently buttoning her pajama top as she did so. "I have emergency rations," she explained.

"Such as?"

"Snickers. Chocolate-covered raisins. Jelly bellys." She plopped back down on the bed, cross-legged again, and began digging through her voluminous leather bag. "I know they're in here somewhere because I replenished my supply at Harrods while we were in London." She glanced at him through her lashes and smiled. "They had the greatest assortment of jelly bellys I've ever seen. Even better than Bloomingdale's. Oh, drat!" she said, upending the purse.

The contents spilled out over the bed—a purse-sized natural bristle brush, a decorative comb and two barrettes, elastic-coated rubber bands, a notepad with a pen attached by a red ribbon, extra pantyhose, innumerable tubes of lipstick and eye color pencils, travel guides and maps, a change purse, an address book and an over-stuffed wallet, old sales receipts, a tin of aspirin, a half-eaten Snickers bar, an unopened bag of colorful jelly bellys with a Harrods label, a gold Cross pen, an empty money clip and a pair of antique gold cuff links.

Samantha froze, her eyes going guiltily to Nick's face. His smile faltered. "What's this?" He sat up slowly, reaching for the cuff links before Samantha could command her muscles to move. "My cuff links? What are you doing with my cuff links? And that Cross pen, it's Terri's, isn't it? Where did you find it?"

Samantha couldn't seem to form the words to answer him. What could she say? Her mind whirled frantically, trying to think of a way to tell him how those things had gotten into her purse without implicating Robbie. An impossible task. She shook her head slightly, unaware that she did so. Unaware, too, that her chaotic thoughts were mirrored in her expressive face, giving her a scared and furtive look.

"Samantha?" he said, puzzled by her reaction.

"Nick, I—It's not what you think it is." She made a helpless, placating gesture. "It's not what it looks like."

"And what does it look like?" he asked carefully. Why was she acting like that? All defensive and guilty? "Samantha?"

"I—It's—"

"Samantha, what is it?"

She shook her head.

The happiness drained out of him, like water whirling down a drain. "Are you some kind of—of kleptomaniac?" he asked, willing it not to be true. But the way she was acting, what else could it be? "Or are you just a common garden variety thief?"

Samantha's eyes widened. "Me?" Never in her wildest dreams did she think he would ever suspect her of such a thing. "Of course not!"

"Then what are these doing in your purse?" He held the cuff links under her nose. "And this?" He flicked the Cross pen with one finger. "And this?" He picked up the money clip and turned it over. "To JCW, with love from CLB," he read aloud. His eyes touched hers again. "JCW? Jeffrey? Is this Jeffrey's money clip?"

"I don't know for sure," she whispered. "I think so."

"You don't know? It's in your purse, how could you not know?"

"Because I—because it—"

"Because why, Samantha?" He felt his control slipping away as he waited for her answer, just as it had slipped away from him when she rocked above him in ecstasy. "How could these things get in your purse if you didn't put them there?"

Because of Robbie, she wanted to say. *Because Robbie stole them and I was going to give them back without anybody knowing.* But she couldn't. She saw her stepbrother in her mind's eye, not as he'd been at dinner, but as he'd been this afternoon—frightened, weeping, looking to her to protect him. *It's all your fault*, he'd said, clinging to her like a child.

And maybe it was. Maybe she had driven him to it somehow. The family psychiatrist they'd had all those years ago had suggested something like that. Not that she was at fault, exactly, but that she might be a contributing factor. "Robbie envies his stepsister," the psychiatrist had said, "he's intimidated by her self-confidence." Maybe he still was. Even if he wasn't, he was still her stepbrother and her friend. She owed him some loyalty. Didn't she? Besides, she had promised.

"Couldn't you just trust me for now?" she asked.

Nick wavered for nearly a full minute. Trust her? Did he dare? He wanted to. Oh, how he wanted to! But how could he trust her when he didn't trust himself? The Gavinos in love were notoriously bad judges of character. His whole family had proved that to him time and again. They lost all control, all good sense. He wasn't going to let that happen to him. And he was going to fight it with everything he had in him if it already had.

"No, I don't think I can." He reached out and grasped her chin in his hand. "How did these things get in your purse, Samantha? And tell me the truth, dammit!" Their eyes locked for a long, charged moment.

"They're Robbie's," she whispered.

"What?"

"Robbie's," she said miserably. "He's got an emotional problem. He gets depressed. Clinically depressed. And he, ah, takes things sometimes."

Nick thrust her chin away from him with a gesture of disgust. "You mean he *steals* things."

"Not deliberately," Samantha hurried to explain. "It's like alcoholism or people who binge on food. He can't help it. The urge comes over him and he shoplifts."

"Shoplifts? You mean this—" he gestured to the things spread out on the bed "—isn't all he's taken?"

Samantha didn't answer but the look on her face was answer enough.

Nick surged to his feet, unaware and unconcerned by his nakedness. Discarded items from her purse rolled across the bed. A tube of lipstick fell to the floor. Nick was unaware of that, too.

He had suspected there was something not quite right about Robbie since the first day in Paris. Before that, if he was honest with himself. He had even intended to call his New York office and have the photographer investigated. But he hadn't. Because he was falling in love with the photographer's stepsister, he'd let it slide. He'd let his growing feelings for her blind him to what was happening right under his nose. As a result, someone in his organization had been shoplifting all over western Europe and he hadn't done a single thing about it.

"Dammit!" He grabbed his discarded robe off the foot of the bed, shrugging into it as he headed for the door.

"Where are you going?"

"To fire Robbie," he said savagely. "And then kick his butt all the way back to New York!"

Samantha sat stock-still in the middle of the littered bed for a shocked moment. He couldn't mean that, could he? She scrambled up, trying to reach him before he got to the door.

"You can't." She grabbed the sleeve of his robe and held on for dear life. "Nick, wait! You can't do that."

"Why the hell not?" he growled, but he stopped.

"Because Robbie needs help and understanding, not someone beating him to a bloody pulp, that's why not. He's not a criminal, Nick. He has a mental health problem and he's not responsible for what—"

"Who's responsible then? You?"

"Me?" How could Nick think she was responsible for Robbie's behavior? "I don't know what you mean, Nick."

"I asked a simple question. I want a simple answer. Are you the one I should hold responsible for having someone like Robbie in the same house with my sister?"

"Robbie's no threat to Marina."

"How do you know that? How do I know that? Marina's emotionally fragile right now. And he was playing up to her at dinner tonight, using her to make you jealous. Who knows if something like that couldn't send her over the edge again?"

"But it wasn't working, Nick," she said logically. "Marina wasn't interested in him and—"

Nick was in no mood for logic. "Dammit, Samantha, you know how vulnerable Marina still is. How easily she's upset. But did you think about that? Did you think about anything but yourself and what you want?"

"Nick!" Samantha backed away from him, tears springing to her eyes at his unfairness.

"Dammit, Samantha!" His fist slammed into the door. He knew he was being unfair and unreasonable but he couldn't seem to help it. He was scared. More scared than he had ever been of anything in his life. "Why couldn't you have told me?"

"Because I knew you'd react just like this!" she flared, her unshed tears drying as if by magic. "Because even with someone like Marina right under your nose—"

"Leave my sister out of this," he snapped.

Samantha ignored him. "I knew you wouldn't understand. That you wouldn't even try to understand," she said furiously, beyond considering what she was saying. "No, damn you, wait!" She grabbed his sleeve again as he reached for the doorknob. "I haven't finished yet, Mr. Holier-Than-Thou-Gavino. Just because you never have any doubts—"

No doubts? Oh, God, he was assailed by them!

"Just because you're some kind of superman who's always in complete control doesn't mean that everybody else is, too. But you can't see that! You can't see how someone could be weak or insecure or just plain afraid. Can you?" She barely paused for breath, she was so caught up in her anger. Anger that was fueled by the guilt she'd carried around with her for the past week— and the strange, closed expression she couldn't read in her lover's eyes. "Well, can you?" she demanded when he didn't answer.

He couldn't answer her. Any answer at all would only pull him in deeper, and he was already floundering in a morass of feelings that he couldn't decipher or separate. Anger, desire, love, regret, fear. He felt helpless and out of control and he hated it. So he shut down, freezing everything behind a wall of implacable will.

"No, of course not," she raged on, trying to get a response, any response, from him. "You have no idea how losing his job would be the worst thing for Robbie right now. How fragile his ego is. How insecure and vulnerable— He's as vulnerable as Marina is, do you know that? Do you care? No, of course you don't care," she answered her own question. "Well, *that's* why I didn't tell you. Because I knew you'd act exactly like you're acting." She stood flushed and trembling, unshed tears standing in her eyes.

"Are you finished?" His voice was quiet, calm and totally emotionless.

Samantha nodded. What else was there to say?

"Fine." He opened the door. "So am I."

11

THE INVITATION was embossed in silver script on heavy emerald card stock, decorated with a silver tassel and scented with *Night Magic* perfume. "You are cordially invited to meet Gavino Cosmetics' Sophisticated Lady," Samantha read for the hundredth time. It had been sent over by messenger that morning with a note from Nick's secretary reminding her that a car would pick her up at four o'clock. There had been nothing from Nick himself. Not a word since he walked out of her bedroom at the Villa Rosa nearly four weeks ago.

"Don't you think you should be getting ready, dear?" Samantha's mother asked, glancing up from the magazine she was skimming. She was already dressed in a chic, six-year-old Chanel suit and a pair of two-tone slingback pumps. "We've got less than an hour before the car is scheduled to be here."

Margaret Spencer's invitation to her soon-to-be-famous daughter's launch party had been delivered two weeks ago and she'd taken the train down from Connecticut especially to attend. She might have her doubts about the Gavino family being the "right kind of people" but she had no doubt at all about the value of their business interests. A recent issue of *Business Week* had done an impressive article on the new cosmetics division, with a sidebar estimating Nick Gavino's personal wealth at "something in the neighborhood of four million."

"Samantha," she said again, prodding her daughter. "Did you hear me?"

"Yes, mother, I heard you," she said listlessly. "There's no hurry. It'll only take me a few minutes to finish getting ready." She'd already done her face, with *Sophisticated Lady* cosmetics, of course. Her thick, silver-blond hair curved to her shoulders, sweeping over one eye from an off-center part.

"Well, I wish you'd hurry, anyway, dear. You know how I hate to arrive late. It's so terribly ill-bred." Margaret gave a ladylike little shudder and flipped a page in the magazine. "The new summer fashions are very nice, aren't they?" she said. "Especially the new Ralph Lauren. He never goes overboard like some of the other designers do."

"Yes, mother." Samantha slipped the invitation into the pocket of her blue kimono wrap and headed for the bedroom. She paused behind the sofa, her eyes on the upswept coil of hair that was almost exactly the color of her own. "Were you ever in love?" she asked impulsively.

Margaret Spencer twisted her head to look over her shoulder at her daughter. "In love?"

"Yes, you know, in love. With a man." She came around the sofa and sat on the arm. "With daddy."

"I was fond of your father," Margaret said, fingering her pearls. "I'd known him all my life. We belonged to the same tennis club. Had the same friends."

"Then why did you get divorced?" She'd heard her father's version but had never thought to ask her mother for hers. Maybe it would prove enlightening. "Did you just grow apart, like he said. Or was it because of Kate?" Kate was Robbie's mother. "Or something else all together?"

"I hardly remember now, it's been so long." Margaret and Samuel Spencer had been divorced since Samantha was six. "I don't believe your father knew Kate back then but perhaps he did."

"Did it tear you apart when he left?"

Margaret laughed lightly. "Tear me apart? Goodness, no. I was more relieved than anything." She looked up at her daughter, staring for a moment into eyes that were as clear and gray as her own. "What's the matter, Samantha?" There was a hint of disapproval in her cultured tone. "Are you having some sort of man trouble?"

"Something like that." She hesitated, wanting to confide in her mother but not quite sure where to start. They had never gone in for cozy mother-daughter confidences.

"It's never a good idea to let oneself get too involved with a man," Margaret Spencer said. "It inevitably gets messy and complicated."

"I know someone who would agree with you entirely," Samantha mumbled.

"What was that, dear?"

"Nothing, Mother." Samantha sighed and got to her feet. "I'm going to go change now. When Robbie comes, let him in, will you?"

Margaret nodded absently, already involved in her magazine again.

SAMANTHA STOOD in front of her closet, trying to work up some enthusiasm for the party. You're the Sophisticated Lady, she told herself. You're going to be famous. And rich. And every man in New York is going to be after you.

Except the only man who mattered.

She pressed her head against the doorjamb of the open closet. "Oh, God, Nick."

He'd cut himself off from her completely, not even bothering to say good-bye to her after storming out of her bedroom at the villa. No, she corrected herself, he hadn't stormed out. She'd have felt better if he had because it would have meant that there was some emotion there, even if it was only anger. He'd swept out of the room like a Roman prince—calmly, coolly, as in control as ever. She hadn't seen him since.

But she would be seeing him today. He was under the same obligation to be at the launch party as she was. She'd have one more chance to . . . to what? He'd made it plain that he didn't want anything to do with her, hadn't he?

Samantha, my love. My sweet love. I love you. I love you. The words came back to her, as clearly as if he were standing beside her, saying them now.

Could he have said them and not meant it? Some men did it all the time. But did Nick?

No, she told herself. There had been no need for him to say things he didn't mean just to get her into bed; she was already there without sweet talk and lies. Nick wasn't the kind of man who lied about his emotions, anyway. He wasn't a man who willingly talked about his emotions at all. No, he had meant them when he said them, all right. But would he lower his guard enough to say them again?

Even if he didn't or wouldn't or couldn't admit he loved her, well, he needed her. And she loved him so desperately she was willing to settle for that. For now.

Oh, who was she kidding? Forever, if that's the way it had to be.

The doorbell rang, interrupting her mind's tortured wanderings. Robbie was here. He'd moved out of the loft when they returned to New York, both of them agreeing that they couldn't continue to live together in light of the way he felt about her. He'd gone into group therapy, a special group made up exclusively of people who shoplifted as a symptom of their depression and low self-esteem. He'd written a short note to Marina, apologizing for the way he'd tried to use her and, much to his surprise, had received an understanding letter in reply. He wasn't well, by any means, but he had made a start.

Samantha reached into the closet, pulling out a sleek emerald-green jacket and slim black skirt that had been purchased weeks ago especially for the launch party. The jacket matched the *Sophisticated Lady* packaging exactly.

She slipped the knee-length skirt on over sheer black stockings and buttoned the form-fitting, collarless jacket to her throat. Large square silver earrings, ornamented with a faux emerald in one corner, adorned her ears. A triangular silver pin with a slash of green crystal running through it like a lightning bolt was fastened to her left shoulder. High-heeled, black suede pumps made her legs look impossibly long and slender. She sprayed herself with a cloud of the *Sophisticated Lady* daytime fragrance, tucked a flat, black patent envelope bag under her arm and took a deep breath. She was as ready as she'd ever be. Pasting a brilliant smile on her glossy lips, she opened the door to her bedroom and stepped out.

Margaret Spencer was already on her feet, waiting. "You look lovely, dear," she said approvingly.

"You're a knockout, Sammie," Robbie added.

"Thanks. Are we ready?"

"The car was already waiting at the curb when I came up," Robbie said.

She took another deep breath. "I guess we're ready, then."

NICK DIDN'T APPEAR to need anyone. He looked exactly as he had at that very first party—a lifetime ago, it seemed. Urbane. Powerful. Confident. In complete control.

He crossed the room to them as soon as she and Robbie and her mother arrived. "Robbie," he said, shaking the photographer's hand. "And this must be Mrs. Spencer." He raised her hand to his lips with continental charm. "I can certainly see where Samantha gets her beauty," he said. Then he took Samantha's hand, tucking it into the crook of his arm, just as he had before. "If you'll excuse us for a moment?" he said politely, leading her to the center of the room. All eyes followed them.

"Ladies and gentlemen, I give you Samantha Spencer, Gavino Cosmetics' Sophisticated Lady," he said, introducing her with almost the same words he'd used before.

But his free hand wasn't covering hers, his eyes weren't smiling with shared laughter, he wasn't looking at her as they stood there, sharing the spontaneous burst of applause that had followed his introduction.

He removed her hand from his arm as soon as he politely could, reaching out to take the champagne glass that someone handed him. Someone else put a glass into Samantha's hand.

"To a successful campaign," he said, looking around the room. He raised his glass to Samantha without really looking at her. "To our Sophisticated Lady, without whom there would be no campaign. To our intrepid production manager, Terri Gunnerson." He lifted his glass in Terri's direction. "To the rest of our production crew, many of whom are unable to be here today. And to Robbie Lowell—" he raised his glass a third time "—the photographer whose talent has made what might have been merely beautiful pictures of a beautiful woman into works of art."

The applause was louder this time and lasted longer.

"Nick, thank you for—" Samantha began, intending to thank him for praising Robbie's work but the whole roomful of people seemed to converge on them all at once.

"Well, Samantha, what do you think?" asked a reporter from *Woman's Wear Daily.*

"Of what?" she said, her eyes following Nick as he moved away from her.

"Of this!" The reporter waved his hand. "Of your pictures."

For the first time since entering the party, Samantha really looked around the room. Images of herself stared back from every corner. There she was, wrapped in dark, sleek sables, looking more glamorous than she ever had in real life as she stepped out of a London taxi—and there, looking chic and successful in a sleek electric blue suit on the busy floor of the New York Stock Exchange.

Other pictures captured her sharing an intimate breakfast with a devastating man on the balcony of a Paris hotel, looking impossibly sexy in black silk pajamas, lazing in a gondola, her fingers trailing in the water as it drifted on the Great Canal of Venice.

"Goodness, is that really me?" She walked up to inspect the poster-sized pictures more closely, astounded at how elegant and ethereal she looked in one, how glamorous and sexy in another, how cool and sporty in still another. She hadn't realized that her range was so great.

"You've all made me look so beautiful." Her voice held a hint of pleased wonder as her eyes swept around the room, trying to find the familiar faces of those who had been on the shoot. "It's like looking at someone else." A smile dimpled her cheeks for a moment. "I think that's called false advertising."

"That's just advertising, period," Terri Gunnerson said, coming over to join the circle gathered around Samantha.

"Well, thank you all, anyway. I could never have looked like that without you." Her eyes sought her stepbrother's. "Especially you, Robbie. They're—" she spread her hands, palms up "—I can't add anything to what Nick said. They're works of art."

"Yeah." Robbie still had a rather dazed look on his face. He shot a quick glance in Nick's direction as if he couldn't believe that the older man had actually praised him. "They are, aren't they?" He looked a bit insulted when everyone laughed at his remark, and then flushed slightly when he realized what he'd said. "Well, they are," he insisted sheepishly.

Samantha linked her arm in his. "Yes, they are. And you should be very proud of them." She drew him away from the crowd that was gathering around the bar and buffet table. "And I'm proud of you, Robbie," she said, squeezing his arm. "Very proud."

"It's all because of you."

"Oh, no, Robbie." Samantha interrupted before he could finish. "It's *your* talent. *Your* photographic genius. You heard what Nick said." They both glanced over to where he was talking to Samantha's mother, politely bending his head to listen to what she was saying. "They're works of art."

"That's not what I meant, Sammie. I mean, well...it's because of you that Nick didn't fire my ass in Italy. It's because of you that I even got the chance for anyone to see what I can do."

"But it's *your* talent." Almost automatically, she began trying to reassure him.

Robbie put his hand over her mouth, silencing her. "Will you quit trying to play big sister for a minute and let me finish?"

Samantha nodded.

"What I've been trying to say is that, well, words aren't really enough, not after what I've put you through, but thank you, Sammie. For everything. For trying to make me believe in myself, for making me realize that I needed help. For making sure that I got that help. No, wait a minute," he said when Samantha opened her mouth again. "I'm not finished. I want to apologize, too." He looked away from her as if struggling with some inner turmoil. "I've acted like a real ass," he said, still not looking at her. "Not just about my—" he hesitated slightly "—problem but about you and Nick." His hazel eyes sought her gray ones. "I know how you feel about him. I've known it from the first. Any fool could see how fascinated you were. And how fascinated he was. Is," he corrected himself with another look at Nick.

She put her hand on his arm. "Robbie, you don't have to say this."

"Yes, I do." He lifted her hand from his arm, taking it in both of his. "I've made the last couple of months pretty miserable for you. I've used our relationship to force you to lie for me."

"Robbie, you didn't force—"

"No, don't try to deny it. I knew exactly what I was doing when I made you promise to cover for me. I was really trying to force you to choose. And I thought, when Nick left Italy the way he did, that I'd won." His grip on her hand became almost painful. "But you were farther away than ever. And you were hurting. For a while that was okay because I was hurting, too, and it only seemed fair. It was only after we got back to New York and I got started in my therapy group that I began to see how wrong I'd been. How selfish." He looked into her eyes, willing her to understand.

She squeezed his fingers.

"It's been a long time coming, Sammie, but I've finally realized that it isn't your fault that I fell in love with you. You didn't ask me to. And it isn't your fault that you don't love me back, either. None of us can choose who we're going to fall in love with."

Samantha didn't know what to say. "I do love you, Robbie," she said finally, her voice soft with compassion. "But like a bro—"

"Yeah, I know. Like a brother." A lopsided smile twisted his mouth, making him look more like his old self than he had in months. "Maybe in a year or two I'll be able to think of you as a sister, too."

"Hey, Robbie," Terri called, waving an arm frantically. "Come over here and have your picture taken."

"In a minute." He reached up and touched Samantha's forehead. "Don't look so tragic, Sophisticated Lady. It'll make wrinkles on that beautiful face of yours."

"Robbie!" Terri's voice interrupted them again. "Come on. You're the new 'boy wonder' of the photographic world."

He grinned. "My public awaits," he said, leaning forward to place a soft, almost brotherly kiss on her cheek. "See ya later, okay?"

"Sure. See you later." She watched him join the group clustered around her Paris pictures. He smiled, nodding at something one of the fashion reporters said to him. Then he laughed, shaking hands with another man. A look of glowing pride and budding self-confidence radiated from him, making Samantha feel like a proud mother.

He's going to be fine, she thought fondly. Six months on the outside and she'd bet he would be calling her Sis and asking for advice on how to handle some girl or other.

But what about me? she thought forlornly, catching sight of Nick as he stood talking to two Japanese gentlemen in business suits.

Nick had tuned her out completely, seemingly effortlessly, sealing himself off behind a wall of detached politeness that she had no idea how to scale. Maybe he didn't love her after all. Maybe he didn't need her, either. Maybe she should just go home and start trying to forget about him.

She snagged her mother, catching her attention as Margaret crossed over to inspect the buffet table. "I'm leaving now, Mother. Do you want to come with me?"

"Now?" She glanced at the trim gold watch on her wrist. "Isn't it a bit early to disappear?" she said disapprovingly. "You are the guest of honor."

"The guest of honor has a screaming headache," Samantha said. "And you don't have to leave now, if you don't want to. I'll just grab a cab." She touched a smooth cool cheek to her mother's. "Enjoy yourself. I'll see you later."

She managed to slip out the door with only her mother and Nick aware that she had gone.

12

NICK SAT in his darkened office, his tie hanging from a mangled knot around his neck, the top two buttons of his shirt undone, staring out over the New York skyline as if it were the most fascinating sight in the world. The launch party was long over, the last of the merrymakers having eventually decided to continue it at some trendy nightspot. It had been a rousing success, by anyone's standards. The fashion forecasters, the ad agency professionals, the movers and shakers of the cosmetic world, had all been wildly impressed. Gavino Cosmetics' *Sophisticated Lady* was off to a running start.

And Nick Gavino was miserable. A huge lump of icy nothing had settled where his heart should have been, sending a freezing numbness all through his body. As much as he hated to admit it to himself, there was only one way—one person—to thaw it.

She had arrived at the launch party exactly on time, looking ravishing and chic in an emerald-green jacket that made her eyes look even more gray in contrast and turned her hair to silver-kissed snow. He'd hurried over to her, practically tripping over himself in his pathetic eagerness. She'd brought him up short with those eyes of hers, turning them on him with a look of cool unruffled serenity and sophisticated poise, as if he were someone she'd met once and couldn't quite remember. He'd hated it.

That cool version of the woman he loved wasn't what he wanted at all. If seeing her again hadn't instantly convinced him of that, talking to her mother, who was an older version of exactly the kind of woman he thought he preferred, certainly had. Margaret Spencer was a chilly harbinger of what Samantha would become if she tried to be what he'd thought he wanted. Beautiful, poised and passionless. An empty, emotionless shell.

Like him. No, he corrected himself. Like he *had* been. He wasn't emotionless now. He was seething with feelings. They stormed inside him like a turbulent sea under an ice floe. He hated that, too.

So, it came down to a question of which he hated worse. Feeling or not feeling. Samantha or no Samantha. Taking a chance on losing himself in love or spending the rest of his sorry life yearning for it.

It was really no contest.

SAMANTHA SAT in her darkened living room, huddled in a corner of her sofa, staring blankly out the uncurtained windows at the roof tops and lights of New York City at night. A blue neon sign glowed atop the building across the street, advertising the location of a currently popular comedy club. The sounds of traffic drifted up on the warm summer air, far enough away to be mildly pleasant. Samantha sniffled, wiping at her eyes with the back of her hand.

Her mother had already been and gone, returning from the party in time to pack and catch her train back to Connecticut. It was probably terribly undaughterly of her, but Samantha was glad to see the last of her mother. It meant there was no one around to make disapproving noises while she ate cookies and cried and generally felt sorry for herself.

She'd been wrong about Nick. Again. He didn't need her. Quite obviously, he didn't need anyone. The only time she'd been right about him was that last, fateful night at the Villa Rosa. He *was* a superman—capable of building empires in a single decade, able to overcome any obstacle by sheer force of will, equipped to deflect any emotion with a steely-eyed glance.

And she loved him in spite of it. Or, maybe, because of it. She could probably be that perverse. Who really knew?

She sniffled again and bit into another Oreo, not even bothering to pry it open and savor the filling first as she usually did. With her nose all congested from crying she wouldn't be able to taste it, anyway. She shoved the rest of it into her mouth, determined to finish the package before she started in on the Rocky Road ice cream. One thing at a time was all she was capable of at the moment.

The doorbell rang.

"Go away," she mouthed, huddling deeper into the corner of the sofa. "Let me eat myself to oblivion in peace."

It rang again.

Robbie, she decided tiredly, probably coming over to see how she was. If she sat very still and quiet, without making a sound, he might think she was out or asleep and go away. She just wasn't up to facing Robbie right now, pretending everything was okay so he wouldn't feel guilty about what he'd done.

The bell rang again—a long, loud, insistent sound, as if whoever it was were leaning on the buzzer and had no intention of going away, no matter how quiet she was.

"All right. All right." Samantha set the half-eaten package of cookies on the sparkling glass coffee table already littered with crumpled tissues and got to her feet. "I'm coming, Robbie. But, dammit, I'm not going to pretend everything is okay." She put her eye to the little spy hole with the ingrained caution of the hardened New Yorker.

Not Robbie.

Her heart started beating double-time.

The doorbell rang again.

Samantha wiped at her mouth with the back of her hand to get rid of any cookie crumbs, ran her palms over her frazzled hair, straightened the lapels of her robe and took a deep breath before opening the door.

"Nick," she said, swinging it open just as he leaned on the bell for the fifth time.

They stared at each other, speechless, for nearly a full minute.

Nick found his voice first. "I need to talk to you, Samantha," he said softly. "Please."

Without a word, she stepped back and let him in. "Would you like a cup of coffee?" she asked politely, twenty-five years of social conditioning coming to her aid without any effort at all despite the fact that she was trembling inside. *Why is he here? What does he want to talk to me about? Oh, Nick!* "I was just about to put a fresh pot on," she lied. "My mother brought me some of her special beans from Connecticut."

"No, no coffee, thanks. Samantha, I—" *What do I say? Where do I start? What do I do to show her I'm willing to take a chance?*

What he wanted to do was wrap her in his arms and forget all about the need for words, but he knew that wasn't an option. Or was it? He eyed her hopefully. No, it definitely wasn't an option, not with this cool-eyed, self-possessed woman. She would want—she *deserved*—an apology and a few explanations first, not to mention a passionate avowal of his undying love.

"Samantha, I—" Damn, he'd never been so tongue-tied in his life! She stood there on the other side of the sofa, wrapped in some sort of bright blue kimono thing, her feet bare, her hair tousled, looking at him like— Hell, he didn't know what she was looking at him like. It was too damned dark in the room. "Do you think we might turn on some lights?"

"Certainly." She moved across the room and flicked on a small reading lamp on the end table beside a cushioned chair. It flooded the chair and the space for two feet around it with light but left her face in shadow.

"May I sit down?"

She extended her hand, palm up, toward the sofa. "Please," she said.

He sat, balancing uneasily on the very edge of the sofa.

Gingerly, Samantha perched on the arm of the chair across from him. "You said you wanted to talk?" she prompted politely. *So talk! Don't keep me in suspense like this!* But he simply sat there, looking at her with those hot-coffee eyes of his as if he'd never seen her before.

She's been crying, he thought, staring at her. For him? For Robbie? For someone else, entirely? He'd walked out on her, and it had been four weeks since he'd seen her last. In the fast-paced life of a beautiful New York model, four weeks was long enough to have found someone else. If she'd been the kind of woman he'd thought he wanted her to be, she would have. But not his Samantha. He hoped.

She jumped up, unable to sit there and endure his silent scrutiny for another minute. She turned her back on him, crossing to the window to stare down into the street. The blue neon sign glowed softly, casting its ghostly light on the patrons who frequented the club below it. The silence stretched between them, tighter, louder, full of unspoken words.

The hell with it, Nick thought savagely, getting to his feet. He'd let his actions speak for him. He simply didn't have the words to tell her how he felt, for the simple reason that he'd never had a need for them before.

She didn't turn as he came up behind her, didn't move as he raised his hands and placed them lightly—oh so lightly—on her shoulders. Encouraged by her acquiescence, he bent his head and touched his lips to her hair like a supplicant at a shrine.

A tentative joy surged through Samantha, as sharp as a knife, as sweet as a forbidden kiss. She closed her eyes against it, fighting the urge to turn around and throw herself into his arms. She'd done that the last time. This time—if there really was going to be a "this time"—she wanted the words first. "You said you wanted to talk, Nick."

"Yes, I do," he whispered. "But I can't seem to remember what I wanted to say." Gently, he turned her to face him. "All I can remember right now is how long it's been since the last time I held you."

She stood very still, staring blankly at the wedge of dark hair revealed by his open shirt collar and the mangled tie still hanging around his neck.

"Samantha," he pleaded. "Look at me. Please."

Her lashes lifted. Their eyes met. Locked. Loved.

Slowly, as if she might bolt and run at the slightest wrong move, he reached out and drew her into his embrace. Forgetting all about the mental conditions she'd just made, Samantha wrapped her arms around his waist and laid her cheek against his heart. Nick sighed like a man released from the gallows and buried his face in her hair, clutching her to him as if she were the one responsible for his reprieve. "Samantha," he whispered, rocking her against him. "Samantha."

They stood like that for a long, silent minute, just holding each other, letting the feeling between them heal their ravaged emotions and sooth their yearning souls. And then Nick drew back, just a little, to look into her face.

"It's been a long time since I kissed you, too," he suggested with a tender, questioning smile.

Samantha tilted her head back, silently, unconditionally, offering him her lips and her love. Their mouths touched, softly at first, tentatively, only half open as they reacquainted themselves with the taste and textures of each other. And then tongues came into play, slowly at first, delicately licking lips and sliding over teeth until, suddenly, his hands were cupping her head and their mouths were sealed together like two frantic halves of the same soul trying to fuse themselves into one being.

"Oh, God, I love you." Nick breathed, lifting his mouth from hers to kiss her cheeks and chin and eyes. "I love you."

Joy—strong, insistent and sure—surged through her. She pressed her hands flat against his back, soothing and arousing at the same time. "I love you, too, darling. I love you, too."

"I'm so sorry," he said between kisses. "So sorry. I reacted like an idiot about Robbie, I know. I should have understood."

"No," she insisted. "I should have told you right away. I should have—"

"But I was afraid," he admitted. "I was afraid of what I felt, of what you made me feel, and I lashed out. I tried to push you away because I was afraid I'd turn into my father if I let myself love you." He was determined to get it all out now that he'd started. "That I'd end up like every other Gavino who's ever been in love—a weak, besotted fool with no self-respect and no self-control."

"No, Nick." Samantha captured his face between his her hands. "Love doesn't make you weak." She stared into his eyes, willing him to believe it. "It makes you strong. I don't know why your father killed himself. Lack of love, maybe, and fear and despair and some macho nonsense about death before dishonor. But it wasn't love that did it. And it certainly wasn't love that caused Marina to try to imitate him. But it *was* love, your love, that saved her. She told me that just knowing you were there, that you still loved her in spite of the mess she'd made of her life, was what pulled her through and made her want to go on living."

"I wish I could believe that."

She pressed a tender kiss on his lips. "Believe it, darling," she said. "It's true." She nestled into him, adjusting her body to his. "Nothing could ever make you weak, Nick. Nothing in this world."

Amazingly, he chuckled. "Oh, I don't know," he said, breathing in the fragrance of her hair. "I'm feeling pretty weak right now."

She tilted her head to look up at him. "Yeah?" She hopped up suddenly and threw her arms around his neck, forcing him to catch her up against him. "You don't feel all that weak to me."

He hefted her slightly, getting a better grip.

"Carry me to the couch," she demanded, nibbling on his ear as he obeyed her. "Now sit down."

He dropped backward onto the wicker sofa with her in his lap. It creaked ominously.

"Don't give it a thought," she said when he frowned down at it. She put her hands on either side of his face, turning it to hers. "Give all your thoughts to me."

His eyes were dark and bright, glowing with love and joy. "Gladly," he said and kissed her.

It escalated quickly, going from tender kisses to demanding ones, from fleeting caresses to frantic fumbling for the skin beneath their clothes, before either of them knew quite how it had happened. They paused for breath, foreheads touching as they stared, bemused and aroused and very much in love, into each other's eyes.

"God, I love you," Nick said, amazed and delighted at how good it felt to say it. "I can't say it enough." He hugged her hard, a silly, besotted grin turning up the corners of his beautiful mouth. "I love you!" He nearly shouted the words. His arms were hard around her, holding her tight.

Samantha laughed in sheer delight and hugged him back, surging upward so that his head was pressed to her breasts. "I know you do, darling. I love you, too."

"You're going to have to be patient with me, you know," he said when she had cuddled back down in his lap.

"Patient, how?" she asked, smoothing down his mangled tie with her palm.

"I'm not very good at love."

Samantha grinned. "Oh, I wouldn't say that."

He pinched her lightly. "Be serious."

"I *am* serious. You're extraordinarily good at love."

"I didn't mean sex."

She kissed his nose. "Neither did I."

He gave her a look of mock exasperation. "Samantha."

"All right." She sat up straight and folded her hands in her lap like a good little girl at Sunday school. The effect was marred somewhat by the way the front of her kimono hung open, revealing the pink crests of her pert breasts, but Nick wasn't about to complain. "I'm serious, okay?" she said. "Now, what is it about love that you think you're not very good at?"

"I'm not good with the words, Samantha. I'm not good with the give and take, and I have trouble trusting my emotions to someone else. I have to learn about sharing and being there."

Her eyebrows rose skeptically.

"Oh, it's all right now. Here, like this, with you safe in my arms and nothing but too many clothes between us. But I'll probably backslide a dozen times a week. I'll panic and clam up when things get too emotional for me to handle and expect you to read my mind. And then I'll get mad when you can't." His eyes were serious as he gazed at her. "I don't want us to live like that, Samantha. I want us to be happy and loving all the time."

She smiled tenderly. "You know a lot more about love than you think you do, Nick. But if it'll make you feel better—" she slipped off his lap and stood up, holding out her hand "—I promise to teach you everything I know."

He put his hand in hers. "You won't give up on me, no matter how I might act sometimes?"

Samantha shook her head, a smile on her face as she stared down at him. "Nope. Not even if you backtrack so far that you try to freeze me out again."

"You'll make allowances for my inexperience?" he asked, only half teasing. "And treat me with gentle understanding?"

"Yes," she said solemnly, tugging on his hand to bring him up beside her.

"And promise to love me forever?"

She nodded, her heart too full to speak. ·

"Is that a guarantee?"

Samantha went up on tiptoe and pressed her lips to his. "An ironclad, no refunds, no excuses guaran-damn-tee," she said. And then she turned and led him down the hall to her bedroom.

COMING NEXT MONTH

Your favorite stories have a brand-new look!

American Romance is greeting the new decade with a new design, marked by a contemporary, sophisticated cover. As you've come to expect, each American Romance is still a modern love story with real-life characters and believable conflicts. Only now they look more true-to-life than ever before.

Look for American Romance's bold new cover where Harlequin books are sold.